Copyright © 2017/2

HAUNTED HOCKIN

MW00451381

ISBN-13: 978-1-940087-23-8

21 Crows Dusk to Dawn Publishing, 21 Crows, LLC

This is a work of fiction. Names, characters, places and incidents either are the product of the author's imagination or are used fictitiously, and any resemblance to any actual persons, living or dead, events, or locales is entirely coincidental. This book was printed in the United States of America.

Before visiting any haunted site, verify location, accessibility and safety. I never recommend venturing into unknown areas in darkness or entering private or public property without prior permission. GPS routes may change or become hazardous. Always check with owners/operators of public and private areas to see if a permit is needed to hunt and to check for unsafe areas. Make sure you follow all laws and abide by the rules of any private or public region you use. Readers assume full responsibility for use of information in this book.

Table of Contents

Hocking County

Vinton County

Table of Contents

Athens County

Table of Contents

Perry County

Fairfield County

Table of Contents

Jackson County

Pickaway County

Ross County

Meigs County

Scioto County

Stories in this book came from these Counties in or near the Hocking Hills Region:

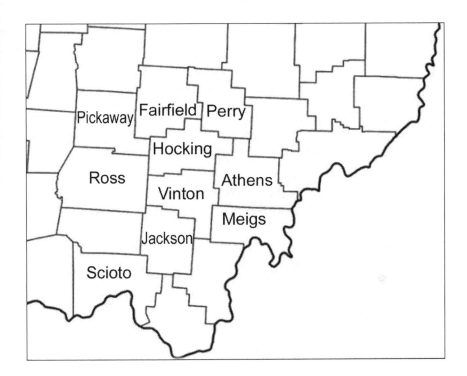

Hocking County

Scotts Creek Falls
13843 OH-93
Logan, Ohio 43138
39.532404, -82.420807

Death Hole

The old road leading to the ford in the creek where it drops off.

Scotts Creek is a stream that makes a lazy run alongside State Route 93 and Scotts Creek Road about six or seven miles before it flows into the Hocking River in Logan. Not far from town, this little tributary has a waterfall. It is here that the water tends to be murky even in the deep of summer when most smaller streams begin to wither to a trickle. It is because the water around the falls is always churning under a great cliff that falls beneath its surface.

The locals have aptly nicknamed this hidden underwater valley *The Death Hole.* Ghosts haunt its surface.

This haunting began in the summer of 1887 when young newlyweds Johannes and Clara Bensonhafer were traveling in a two-horse wagon along Scotts Creek Road with a heavy load of wheat and heading to the local mill in Logan. As they neared the town, it was decided that the horses needed to stop for water. They pulled the team off and along an old ford, driving the horses toward the edge. In moments, the horses, instead of stepping into an expected shallow pool of dingy creek, plunged forward, pitching the couple into the water and dragging the wagon with them. Clara and Johannes immediately drowned. A man who had passed them as they turned toward the creek heard the awful clatter of the wagon hitting the stream and the cries of the panicked horses. He returned to silence and finding nothing of the couple and their horses but a basket and hat floating on the surface, Johanne's jacket on the shore, and bubbles issuing from the water. All had drowned.

The Death Hole on Scotts Creek.

Shortly after the incident, those passing the spot where the couple and the horses came to their death, began seeing strange sights and hearing odd sounds. When nobody else was around, the grind of wagon wheels swept forth from the empty stretch of road by The Death Hole. Soft chatter of a man and woman drifted past with an occasional soft whinny of a horse. Some would see the dark outline of a wagon with two people riding rigid in the seats. The ghostly entourage would slip off the road and to the bank near the falls. Then there were the screams of horses as the phantom team descended into the deep depths of Scotts Creek and disappeared into the nothingness below.

These two images were taken in succession at Scotts Creek above the falls. I enlarged the 2nd. If you look closely and below each arrow, you can see a woman on the left, a man in the center carrying another man over his shoulders and a team of horses on the right. Where the arrow at the bottom points upward, someone is lying on the ground with head resting on arms.

Collison Cemetery
Near Hocking Hills KOA
29150 Pattor Road
Logan, Ohio 43138
39.468286,-82.489368

A Haunting at Blackjack

Aryanne's grave is in Collison Cemetery.

Years ago, there was a town called Blackjack where the Hocking Hills KOA campground stands today between Logan and Old Man's Cave. Only a few homes remain along with an aged cemetery, settled on a hillside once John Collison's property. A ghostly girl walks from the area where the old homestead once stood, now the camp office.

She makes her way through the campground, along a little dirt path, and into the cemetery.

Most believe that the restless ghost is a local farmer's daughter, 16-year-old Aryanne Hutton, who was buried there in 1893, for it is near her grave that the figure pauses. Along the way, people have heard her whisper, "Come." and "I am leaving." It appears as if she wishes those who hear her words would follow her. But where she goes, nobody knows because she then vanishes.

Cedar Falls
OH-374
Hocking Hills State Park
Logan, Ohio 43138
39.418819, -82.524742
Near A-Frame Bridge along trail
Trailhead Parking:
39.418280, -82.526563

Welcome to Hell

During the annual Winter Hike, the old Road to Hell from Cedar Falls to Ash Cave is the most desolate, eerie section.

In the early 1800s, a grist-mill powered by the waters of Queer Creek sat on the rim of Cedar Falls. Nearby was a massive beech tree with words engraved deeply in its ancient trunk, "This is the road to hell, 1782."

The beech was along a dark, tree-covered trail that worked its way deep into the gorge. It was often used by Shawnee and Delaware traveling to Chillicothe around the time tempers were high between settlers and Indians. It was speculated often by those visiting the mill in days long past that captive pioneers had been marched along this rugged path strewn with boulders and murdered along the route. After one particular raid, a trapper was captured by the Indians and camped beneath its wide canopy one night. As the story goes, his beard was pulled from the roots and he was burned and branded with pine knots, an especially hot piece of wood. After suffering untold agony, he was able to escape into the wilderness and towards what is now Ash Cave, but not before etching those words into the tree. On moonless nights, the screams of others who did not escape are heard issuing from the valley where the mill once stood not far from the A-Frame bridge along the Cedar Falls trail.

Cedar Falls. Where the Queer Creek waters work their way past and where an old beech tree at a mill once marked the final path of settlers captured by Native Indians and awaiting their death. If you walk the bridge above Cedar Falls and look down, you may see remnants of an old mill.

Simcoe Creek/Valley
Off Tick Ridge Road and
Along Old Sudlow-Lee Road
39.424735, -82.370202
Pull-off along Tick Ridge:
39.424530, -82.380275
Trail is old Sudlow-Lee Road, rugged
and a 2-mile round-trip. This is mostly
Wayne National, but there is marked
private property along the trail.

Ghost of Simcoe Valley

In the mid-1800s, there was a young girl named Lucille Simpson who lived on a large plantation in Virginia. Her only brother died at a young age, so her parents indulged her with nearly anything she wanted. Few children lived in the vicinity of her home, so she played almost every day with the overseer's son, Robert, who lived in a tidy cottage not far from the plantation owner's mansion. The position of overseer had been fulfilled for many years by Robert's father, as had it been by his grandfather when Lucille's grandfather had farmed the land. As the two grew older, this friendship bloomed, and the two became secret sweethearts.

Robert worked with his father during the day, managing the plantation and also ran errands for Lucille's father. Knowing his overseer's hard-working reputation and noting the son's competency, Lucille's father hired Robert as a clerk and bookkeeper in the Simpson Plantation. Robert did remarkably well, and all went smoothly until Lucille's mother began to suspect something, and upon trailing them one evening, caught them speaking sweetly together.

She brought it to her husband's attention, and the man questioned his daughter, who happily confessed the love she had for Robert and asked for her father's blessing to wed. Simpson was quite furious as he had great plans for her to marry someone of equal wealth and prominence. No child of his would marry a common hireling!

Immediately, Simpson fired both the father and the son from their household duties and barred them from his property. He prepared to send his daughter to live with relatives for a short time until things cooled between the couple. Yet, even as the Simpsons made plans to send Lucille away, she and Robert met secretly. While Lucille was out riding alone in the meadow, she was thrown from her horse one morning. It was the week of her departure to stay with an aunt, and for days she lay unconscious.

When Lucille finally awakened, it was nearly Thanksgiving, and in gratitude for his daughter's health, Simpson decided to throw a grand party. In his delight at having his daughter recover from her accident when she asked that her beloved childhood friend Robert attend, the father let his guard down and consented.

At the party, Lucille and Robert immediately found each other. Simpson was well aware of the couple chatting a little too closely, but over the week between his daughter's request to invite Robert and the night of the party, he had come up with a rather devious plan to rid his daughter of the young man once and for all. Or at least curtail the silly idea of a marriage between the two long enough he could find a more suitable match for his only child.

On that same night, he invited the couple into his office and told Robert that he would consent to a marriage on three conditions. They would postpone a wedding for exactly four years. The two could not see each other during the four years, and Robert must leave the plantation.

Simpson also required that Robert make enough money to generously support Lucille by the time he returned. The old man was able to appear sincere enough about the pact that young Robert thought he just needed to prove his worth to them. Regardless, the couple had no choice but to relinquish to Lucille's father's terms.

Robert packed his bags and set off searching for a job, and a means to make his fortune. During this time, southeastern Ohio had coal, iron, and railway boomtowns due to the wealth of mineral lands. Word spread far and wide of an Englishman who decided to invest his riches on American soil and bought a great amount of land in the area around Raccoon Creek. He built many houses along soon-to-be-busy streets for workers and named the little town after himself, Zaleski. The area was flourishing in iron and coal, and the Marietta & Cincinnati railway went right through Zaleski. Robert heard of the ability to make a lot of money there and worked his way to Ohio and this up-and-coming community with many budding enterprises. When he got to Zaleski, the furnace, coal, and mining company quickly snatched him up for the bookkeeping skills he had learned under Simpson's tutelage.

For almost three years, Robert worked successfully, and his salary was plentiful. But then, Zaleski died in England, and his investments in the company town were lost. Most businesses closed, and Robert lost his job. Undaunted, the young Virginian knew that he was close to the amount of money he needed to earn to prove himself a worthy husband for Lucille. If he scrimped, found himself a meager place to stay, and worked another job, he could make up the final amount of cash to wed his sweetheart and make his way back to his home. A man named Shank would provide that income. He was a collier, a maker of charcoal for fueling the iron furnace at Union Furnace 16 miles from Zaleski.

Shank was a seedy character and a known thief living in a remote area of an oak and hickory forest, which he cut to make the charcoal. Robert found work with him when it seemed scarce everywhere else after the closing of the Zaleski businesses. They lived in a dilapidated shack with another worker far outside town in a hollow with a stream, Simcoe Creek, running through it.

Union Furnace.

Making charcoal, the burned wood residue that fired the furnace, was hard and dirty work. It required cutting a large amount of timber and stacking a pile about 12 feet tall over a pit, leaving a small chimney in the center for ventilation. A worker would light the top of the chimney with burning coals from another fire. Once the pile was burning, it was covered with leaves and dirt. The woodpile would burn for about a week, leaving nothing but charcoal which was raked and allowed to cool before being loaded into wagons and taken to the furnace. But the thought of returning home to keep his pledge to his Lucille the following year kept Robert's mind occupied while he earned his meager pay.

Simcoe Valley and creek.

Robert would often pat the purse on his belt, which held the key to his future, smiling softly, feeling soothed with the notion he would soon be with Lucille. This habit was often observed by Shanks, who eyed the pocket hungrily.

When the time came close for the four years to end, Robert wrote to Lucille divulging that he would be home the next Thanksgiving to take her hand in marriage as he had earned enough money to seal the pact with her father. Lucille was ecstatic as she had remained true to her sweetheart, and she had begun to make arrangements to receive Robert at the plantation.

Then one dark, stormy night in mid-November, Shanks ordered Robert to go with him to tend to the midnight rounds checking to see if the charcoal pits were burning properly. Armed with shovels and lanterns, the two set off. However, only Shanks returned to the cabin. As this was not common, the other worker asked Shanks why Robert had not returned. Shanks had replied that one of the pits was not burning, so he had stayed to tend it.

Robert never returned, and Shanks disappeared not long after. Most in the community thought that Shanks had murdered the young man for what he had in his purse, then threw his body into the charcoal pit.

And what became of poor Lucille? When Robert never returned, she wrote a letter to the manager of Union Furnace. He told her the awful news, yet she always believed her sweetheart was alive and would someday return. When the Civil War broke out, her father joined the southern troops. A Union soldier killed him with a bullet to the chest during a skirmish. A battle played out at the plantation, and cannons destroyed it. Having no place to go and still grieving for Robert, Lucille went to work in a hospital, fell sick, and died. Whether Lucille haunts some old, southern Civil War hospital grounds is not known. Nor do we know if her father returns to the plantation to grieve the choices he made. However, I do know the ghostly apparition of Robert is around. Travelers passing the area of the old charcoal pits in Simcoe Valley have seen a mysterious form of a man ooze up from the earth, then slowly trudge to the place where the shack belonging to Shank once stood. Then it disappears.

Simcoe Valley and the creek. Simcoe Creek runs through Wayne National and private lands until it flows into Raccoon Creek in Starr.

Happy Hollow
Laurelville, Ohio 43135
Drive-along: 39.47251,-82.689439
to
39.441529,-82.692769

Dripping Wet

Not far from Rock House, Happy Hollow Road runs from Thompson Ridge Road to State Route 56. It is a little more than a two-mile drive on gritty backroads with houses dotting the valley. Happy Hollow has a ghost. Back in the mid-1900s, folks who lived there would get a frightening glimpse of the spirit of a middle-aged man dressed in wet clothing. He showed up randomly along Happy Hollow Road, on stairways and porches. One girl even saw him on her cellar steps and stood there too frightened to move. By the time she drew enough courage to call for her mother, he had vanished. Most believe he came from the years when Happy Hollow was a coal mining community.

Old Baptist Cemetery
16993 Keister Road
Rockbridge, Ohio 43149
39.489701,-82.597539

Sometimes the Ghosts You Seek Are Far Less Scary Than the Company You Keep.

Old Baptist Cemetery.

It appears that the Old Baptist Church/Kelch Cemetery has held spirits in its grasp for an awfully long time. It probably even had some of Hocking County's earliest ghost hunters stop in for a visit to satisfy their sense of adventure. But of the many things most ghost hunters have learned to recognize, there are two things you can rely upon: One, ghosts do not always show up when you want them to reveal themselves. Two, sometimes the dead ghosts you seek are far less scary than the live company you keep. At least, that is how it appears in The Democrat Sentinel in the autumn of 1909.

The little village of Gibisonville witnessed a very exciting scene last Sunday night. As some of the boys from the west end have been relating a legend about a ghost which is to be seen in a grave yard about one and a half miles west of the village; some of the ladies of the village determined to come to the boys aid. So last Sunday night the ladies made preparations to stay the fiery demon. The legend relates that the ghost appears about half after nine o'clock, but about half past seven the brave heroines could wait no longer, so all being in readiness, away went the entire bevy of ladies and boys for the grave yard to annihilate Mr. Ghost. Some were carrying axes, some knives, some ropes and last but not least came Rosa Raymond with the boot jack. All went well until the western limits of the town were reached when the boys became afraid and fell in the rear and by the time Wood's grove was reached some of our young pedagogues and tool dressers became so afraid that they turned and ran home as fast as their weary limbs would carry them, but nevertheless on pressed the brave ladies followed by a few of the boys until about half a mile from the grave yard, when of a sudden the ladies halted to rest saying they were too tired to go any farther, but lucky for the ladies they were on an elevated place where they could see the home of Mr. Ghost.—

But as it was not yet time for him to appear our heroines suggested the evening be spent in playing games and telling ghost stories until the time of his arrival. When at last the time of his arrival approached the ladies began to watch for Mr. Ghost, but lucky for him, he failed to appear and the ladies were forced to return without having reached the goal, but the results of the evening are almost tragic, for when they were forced to return without seeing Mr. Ghost, Rosa Raymond became so enraged that she began beating Homer Moore over the head with her boot jack. We are sorry to say, but Mr. Ghost is still at large and any one wishing to know anything farther of him can find out by calling on either Mrs. Wm. Moore, Velva Brashares, Goldie Evans or Rosa Raymond or by going to the home of the above named Mr. Ghost. One Who Knows. **The Democrat-Sentinel., Logan, Ohio November 18, 1909.**

Old Man's Cave
Hocking Hills State Park
19852 OH-664
Logan, Ohio 43138
39.434686, -82.541574
Trailhead and Parking:
39.436310, -82.539207

The Old Man of Old Man's Cave

Old Man's Cave (also once known as Dead Man's Cave): Old Man's Cave is a popular tourist attraction in southeastern Ohio featuring a hiking trail that winds through a long, tree-lined gorge with cliff edges, waterfalls, and unique rock formations.

There once was a quiet town between Logan and South Bloomingville called Cedar Grove. It was settled near a sandstone gorge with a meandering stream called Cedar Creek that ran beneath tall cliffs. These cliff walls were covered with recess caves of all shapes and sizes, with one standing out as the largest and called Old Man's Cave.

Just as people like to hike the gorge today, in the early 1900s, it was not uncommon for sightseers to walk the paths beneath the huge hemlocks and view the waterfalls. Back then, though and illegal today, when the area was privately owned, much wilder, and fewer people visited, it was also common for locals to set up ropes on the cliff walls and swing across the wide expanse of the creek below. It was much to the delight and awe of the tourists traveling on the trail beneath.

Old Man's Cave about the time of the story.

One afternoon, two young men by the names of Kreig and Hillis had set up a rope near Old Man's Cave, descending until they were about 50 feet from the creek water. They took turns swinging, basking in the applause from onlookers until Kreig saw a peculiar old man with white hair, gray beard, and wearing old-fashioned leather clothing strolling along the trail. He carried an ancient rifle on his right shoulder, and by his side, a large hound kept stride. Kreig pointed it out to Hillis, who was descending the rope. As Hillis began to swing, the old man stopped and seemed as absorbed in the antics as those milling around the creek. After a short while, the old man appeared to lose interest.

He continued up the trail and into the cave, and as he reached the entrance, he passed a young couple seated on a rock engaged in pleasant conversation.

Cliff over Lower Falls and Cedar Valley Creek where Kreig and Hillis were swinging on the rope. The old man was seen entering on the platform of rock left of the waterfall.

Kreig was still watching with great fascination when he saw the couple turn their heads toward the man as if they had just noticed him. With that, the girl threw her palms to her lips and fell in a faint! Suddenly, those below were either in an uproar, appearing frightened and scurrying around or staring in awe at the old man. Krieg's eyes went from the scene below and then to the old man who had slipped into the large recess cave. Then unexpectedly, the old man and his dog sunk into the sand at the bottom, vanishing.

There was a certain mystery as to where this old ghost originated. From the testimonies of those hailing from the town of Cedar Grove, the old man was discovered many years ago by two young boys who lived in the town and were exploring the valley and its many nooks and crannies.

Growing bored after climbing one boulder after another, they built a small fire within a large recess cave that overlooked a valley of hemlocks and craggy rocks.

One of the boys, the younger of the two, was uncertain about visiting this particular cave. It was rumored to be haunted. Some had heard the low baying of a hound at night there, but when they searched for the dog, it could never be found. The boys had only been inside the cave a few minutes when the crunch of footsteps on leaves and sand forced them to look up from the flames. An old man and a large, white dog, staying close to the man's side, walked past them. The man had a long, gray beard, old-fashioned clothing, and leather moccasins. He carried an antique rifle over his shoulder. The man appeared to be interested in the back of the cave. He paced back and forth near the edge of the far rocks and, upon coming to a standstill, peered intently at a shallow depression in the sandstone earth. Then both the man and the dog vanished into the depression as if they had not been there at all!

Eagerly, the boys sought help from some local adults at Cedar Grove, investigating the place the old man had disappeared. With mattocks and shovels, a small crew of men removed rocks and dug out the hollow in the cave's sandstone floor. They exposed two sets of bones—a man and a dog, an old flintlock rifle with the date of 1702 etched into the wood, and some cooking pots. There was also a scratching in the stone that stated the man's name as Retzler and the date of death as 1777. For a long time, many travelers would come to visit to see the remains inside the cave they dubbed Dead Man's Cave or Old Man's Cave. They would stare down at the old bones and wonder who the man and dog had once been. Some would hear the baying of a hound dog far away, and rumors prevailed that the ghostly dog returned, but for what reason, they did not know.

After a while, the bones disappeared. The curious stopped coming, and the story faded away except for a few living in the community, who brought it up once in a while when lingering outside the grocery store.

One late autumn night not too long ago, a park ranger listened intently to the sound of a dog howling deep in the gorge. Occasionally, dogs from the scattering of homes nearby strayed from their backyards. They usually found their way home, but this particular dog sounded like a hunting hound, and the frantic bay most certainly meant it had treed a raccoon. It could mean that poachers were hunting in the park.

The ranger snatched up his flashlight and worked his way down the rugged trail and into the gorge. He followed the sound of the dog, filtering out the splash of a waterfall and the crunch of sandstone at his feet. But even while he got closer to the hound's yowling howls and threw the beam of his flashlight upward, he could see little in the fog flowing up along the rock cliff. He saw no dog in the darkness. And yet, the howls got louder and louder until they seemed to be circling him just out of reach. He whipped his flashlight around in a circle, then just as suddenly as the dog's baying came, it ceased.

For years, many have heard the baying of a phantom dog within the gorge and cave area called Old Man's Cave. Its presence is explained like this—

Before the settling of the towns of Logan and Cedar Grove, some trappers lived along Cedar Creek, a stream that worked its way through a deep sandstone gorge. These men made their home in modest one-room cabins or animal-skin tents abutting the small caves within the valley. They made a living selling the pelts of the many fur-bearing creatures like otter and fox that roamed the region at the time.

As their jobs required them to travel far into the wilderness, they were gone for many days at a time. One winter, upon returning from a seasonal hunt, neighbors noticed that one particular trapper named Retzler, who made his home in a cave outcropping along with his dog Harper had not been seen in quite some time. The usually heavily-traveled path to his abode was overgrown, and there was no sign of his faithful hound who bayed whenever someone neared the camp.

After taking the footpath that led to the cave, they lifted the flap of his leather-hide tent and peered inside. Before them lay the dead trapper along with his old hound dog dead by his side. They carefully lifted the limp bodies of the man and dog and placed them in a shallow hole they had dug in the back of the cave and covered them with sand.

Ash Cave
Hocking Hills State Park
OH-56
South Bloomingville, Ohio 43152
39.395993,-82.545927

Pale Lady of Ash Cave

Ash Cave—

Hikers have seen the ghost of a young woman dressed in 1920s clothing along the trail that winds its way to the Ash Cave waterfall. She peers from behind trees and tags along on guided night hikes, easing back just far enough to appear like one of the group until she fades away.

On one particular night hike, park naturalist Pat Quackenbush noted a straggler in his group of hikers. As was customary on the walks he led, Pat would stop six or seven times along the trail, pointing out plants and wildlife.

Pat had been a naturalist for well over 40 years; he knew the tricks of the trade. He learned early on to make a routine of silently taking a headcount of those in the group when he stopped to make sure nobody had gotten left behind in the dark. As Pat paused at a beech tree for his seventh and final stop, he began to count out his twelve hikers. With a flush of uncertainty, he realized there were thirteen—somehow, he miscalculated the last six times, or someone had joined the group. He also noted that this thirteenth hiker was deathly pale and dressed in a feed sack dress common in the 1920s.

Pat swallowed hard, then turned to the group. He may have been a naturalist a long time, but he would do something he had never done before on a hike—he asked the hikers before him if they could see a mysterious shadow in the rear of the group. Each turned with uncertainty, and some gasped. With that, the shadow took a couple of steps and vanished. Everyone in the group saw the ghost!

Naturalist Pat Quackenbush leading a hike in Ash Cave. I think the spirit in the cave must be fond of him. One time, while I was on a night hike as a volunteer, I was assigned to be the last hiker to make sure no one was left behind. A good friend of Pat's, Gary Bergstrand, hiked the end with me and we struck up a quiet conversation just before Pat ended his talk at this location. I heard a loud "SHHH!" Thinking that it was my imagination, I turned to Gary and asked him if he heard the odd sound. He chuckled and said, "Yep, I think we just got shushed by a ghost!"

Ash Cave
Hocking Hills State Park
OH-56
South Bloomingville, Ohio 43152
39.395993,-82.545927

The Drummer

Ash Cave—where ghosts lurk—and Naturalist Pat passed on an amusing story of one that likes to play tricks on the rangers—

All the areas at Hocking Hills State Park close at dusk because the trails are near sheer cliffs with edges not visible in the black of night. When darkness comes, the park rangers make the rounds in their cruisers of all the different hiking trail parking lots. They verify the lots are clear of cars. If they find a vehicle after dark, they drag out their flashlights and take a walk along the trail, searching for trespassers along the way, perhaps calling in search and rescue workers for hikers possibly lost in the forest.

Years ago, a park ranger making his nightly rounds heard the sound of drums coming from Ash Cave as he sat in his cruiser with the window rolled down. It would not be the first time someone had illegally snuck into the cave area after hours to try to find a spiritual connection. The ranger sighed and got out of his vehicle, setting off down the dark trail. The closer he got, the louder the drum seemed to get. As he came to the point where the sound had issued and shined his flashlight into the darkness, the drumming stopped. No one was there.

After a thorough search, he turned at the far steps to leave, thinking the drummer had snuck up the trail and left. Even before he set foot on the concrete path out of the cave, the drumming began again, but this time in the opposite direction. There was no way that someone could have made it from one side of Ash Cave to the other without the ranger seeing them cut past him. Undaunted, the ranger did a second thorough search from the back steps to the entrance. Again, he found nothing.

Knowing that there had to be more than one person back there, he got on his radio and called for backup, deciding the only way to catch the tricky trespassers was to have someone come from the opposite direction and trap them between. At the time, radio service was still spotty in the cave. When he called for backup, the second ranger at the office could not make out exactly what he was saying. Believing that the ranger at the cave was in grave danger, he rushed to his car and sped to Ash Cave, lights flashing and sirens wailing. The ranger in Ash Cave, hearing the sirens coming down State Route 56 and pulling into the front parking lot, thought that surely there was something horrendous happening at the park entrance. Just as he started to step forward to make his way to the lot, he heard a voice next to him say, "Shhh, someone's coming."

When he wheeled around, nobody was there. He bolted down the concrete walkway and stopped out-of-breath just short of the second ranger running from his cruiser toward him. It did not take long to figure out there was no need for urgency in either situation. The two got a chuckle out of the event, and hearing no more drumming after a length of time, prepared to leave. As the two began to drive off, the sound of drums had begun again.

Park volunteer, Teri Downard, plays a traditional drum in Ash Cave at an historical event.

The ghostly sounds of Indian drums have long echoed off the recess cave walls, leftover remnants of earlier years when used by Shawnee and Delaware as a shelter, and in some cases, for burials. But drums are not the only noises heard within the cave. In the 1900s, Sunday camps were held here—there is a large, flat rock just outside the cave called Pulpit Rock where ministers would stand to preach for hours to their congregations. One time, while running a recorder during a night hike in the cave, I caught the distinct sound of a large church choir singing.

Early church service in Ash Cave.

**Conkles Hollow
State Nature Preserve**
*24132 Big Pine Road
Rockbridge, Ohio 43149
39.453210, -82.573017*

Conkles Hollow Creepers

Conkles Hollow—lower trail.

Just a little off Big Pine Road in an area that has never been more than sparsely habited, there is a dark hollow. Few people have ever lived there long because of the strange happenings within. Deep moans issue from the bowels of the valley, and on certain nights, screams are heard there.

Three men were murdered here, and it is their voices carried with the wind. Their story has been passed on as this—

During the mid-1700s, flatboats carried families along the Ohio River and the many smaller rivers, searching for a place to settle. There were many fights between the settlers and Shawnee, Wyandot, and Delaware over the land, and attacks on travelers were common. One such group of warriors set out one day to rob flatboats as they came through a narrow, shallow pass along the Ohio River. Once they raided the passengers, they would flee into the unsettled areas of the wilderness that is now the Hocking Hills, pausing long enough to secret their stash in the many small caves of the region.

After several such raids, word traveled about the dangerous and shallow pass where Indians ambushed boats. Some voyagers tried to avoid the pass along the river altogether, while others had no choice, with the large number of possessions they carried, to take the chance they might be waylaid. One expedition was especially fearful of taking the route. They had brought with them all they owned within the boat and among their possessions was a chest filled with many silver coins.

The fearful settlers developed a plan to elude the Indians at this point on their journey. They sent one flatboat ahead with the women, children, and their goods. Just behind would be a posse of men, horses, and guns in a second boat laying in wait and ready to stop the thieves.

On this particular trip, a band of three Indians hijacked the boat. As the warriors seized upon their treasures and opened the chest filled with coins, they delighted in their good luck, but they failed to question why there were no men among the boat passengers until it was too late. Then, the second flatboat with the men and weapons rounded the bend in the river and came upon the thieves.

The posse landed their boat, jumped to their horses, and grabbed their guns to give a chase. They pursued the three warriors relentlessly for days. At some point, the three Indians, believing they had outrun the posse, slowed as they came into a dark valley between two high hills with a small stream running between them. They rested there a day, stuffing their loot into the nooks and crannies of the sandstone cliff walls, handfuls of coins thrust within and all the way back to the end of the narrow creek valley where they could go no farther as it ended in a sheer cliff wall. There they stopped and readied to leave. But not before the thieves heard the sound of horses huffing in the cool, damp air. One Indian looked back and, realizing they had trapped themselves within the hollow, prepared to fight, but the settlers outnumbered them. There was no escape, and the posse murdered the men within the hollow.

Conkles Hollow ends into a wall of rocks that trapped the Indians.

The settlers found some of the stolen goods, but no one ever recovered the many silver coins. Even though a thorough search was made within the hollow, their whereabouts were a mystery. The place almost immediately became a most terrifying area to visit from dusk to dawn.

Moans and groans swept out from the hollow, and ghosts played pranks on those walking within as if they wanted to keep them out.

According to one of the volunteers who helps with the state park activities, strange things do occur within the hollow. She was setting up Tiki bamboo torches along the trail with several young volunteers so visitors could see the path during a night hike at Conkles Hollow. It was a new moon night and very dark. The crew had yet to light the torches, waiting until it was completely dark outside. The four dawdled at a small cave in the bend of the trail and readied with rechargeable lighters and matches to fire up the torch wicks—"When we felt it was dark enough, we all picked a torch to light but as hard as we tried, we could not get any of them to light," she divulged. "Every time we lit a match, it was like a puff of someone's breath blowing it out. Every time we flicked the lighter, it simply would not give us a flame. We had to stagger blindly all the way back to the parking lot in the pitch-black for more matches. All the while, it was deathly quiet around us except a low, hushed whisper we prayed was the creek. Not even the sound of crickets or a deer bumbling around in the leaves in the dark came to our ears. We returned, and suddenly, the old lighters seemed to work and the crickets and birds started chirping again." The night hike went on as planned. However, that same little group of help never volunteered to walk back through Conkles Hollow after dark again!

Tinker's Cave
Wayne National Forest
12318 Burton Hill Road
New Straitsville, Ohio 43766
39.546255, -82.226422
(Watch for gravel pull off. Rugged
trail is on the same side as pull-off.)

Legend of the Dead Horse Thief

Horse Thief Cave.

A man and horses haunt an ancient rock shelter off a lonely stretch of dirt-gravel road at the head of a deep valley. He died many years ago and the reason for this haunting might have something to do with the dead man's dirty deeds in life—It was late one afternoon in the mid-1800s when a lone farmer herded his goats into the back yard of the Buntz House hostel in Logan. The farmer told the inn owner that he had come to town to sell a herd of his goats.

He needed a place to stay for the night, but he could not afford the full night's stay up front. He assured the hostel owner that he would pay half now and the rest in the morning and after he sold the goats. As an act of goodwill, he also suggested that the owner could lock the gates with the goats inside his yard as insurance he would not leave without paying.

The farmer was quite charming and convincing, so the owner agreed to the arrangement, received half the payment, and locked the goats inside the yard. The next morning, however, the goats and farmer had vanished without paying what was due. Only several wooden planks lying askew in the backyard threw light on how the thief had made his escape—he had placed boards up and over the wooden fence so the goats could clamber over in the dark of night, and he could steal away without unlocking the gates. The farmer was not a farmer at all, but a well-known thief named Shep Tinker who had stolen someone's goats and needed a place to hide for the night while he fled.

> —On another occasion, Tinker was riding through the country one Sunday, and, on passing a church, was mistaken for a minister expected to arrive that day. He was warmly welcomed and taken to the church. There he preached a sermon and was on his way not long afterward. **The Sunday Messenger, Sunday June 25, 1953. Logan Scene of Famous Horse Thief's Exploits**

Old newspapers would often recall Shep Tinker swindled business owners and terrorized farmers by stealing their animals all over nearby counties where his well-to-do family had their farm. He hid the livestock in the many caves of the region until he could move them to northern Ohio to sell there.

Many stories were told of his exploits, and it was rumored Shepherd Tinker helped Confederate soldiers, led by John Morgan, during their raids through Ohio by giving his men horses stolen from the town of Logan. He spent time in prison off and on. Once, he even charmed a girl, whose job was to bring food to the prisoners, into helping him escape by stealing the warden's keys.

The cave of the dead horse thief.

Another time, he stole a completely black horse belonging to Doctor James Dew. Doctor Dew, upon seeing Shep Tinker sneak off with his horse, took off after Tinker. As darkness came, Doctor Dew had nearly caught up with Tinker, but realizing he was about to be overtaken, Tinker bound the muzzle of the horse with a white cloth and turned the horse around until he was heading toward Doctor Dew. In the darkness, Doctor Dew called out to Tinker and asked if the man had seen a rider with a black horse. Tinker said, "Yes, I did! He went thataway!" He pointed Doctor Dew in the direction he had come. The doctor took off again after his stolen horse, not realizing until later he had been tricked by the horse thief!

Shepherd Tinker disappeared after the Civil War. Locals always said that Shep stole horses from the wrong farmer and ended up on the short end of a noose right in the very cave where he hid most of his stolen animals and the large rock shelter that bears his name, Tinker's Cave. It also holds his ghost and the ghosts of the horses he had stolen. Hikers have heard muffled whinnies and shuffles of hooves inside the cave and the mumbles of Shep boasting about the thousands of horses he stole.

Falls Township
Logan, Ohio 43138

Falls Township Screamer

OH-93 and Maysville-Williams Road. Near the old drilling site.

Sometime in September of 1910, on the farmland owned by J.W. Williams, a well was drilled for oil about a mile west of Gore by a contracting company owned by John Griffin. There were four workers on the job, two drillers, and two tool dressers. When they changed shifts at midnight, one of the men returned to tighten a piece of equipment. He slipped, fell into the belt, and made a blood-curdling scream of agony before he died. Passersby still hear his scream echoing along the quiet roadway.

Rock House
Hocking Hills State Park
OH-374
Laurelville, Ohio 43135
39.496623,-82.621307

In the Garden

There is a sandstone cave with a tunnel-like passage at Hocking Hills State Park. It is best known as Rock House. Within, those with a keen eye can find small squares excavated into the earth that were troughs dug by early inhabitants of the area to catch water for drinking. Old-timers have long passed down legends that robbers once used the cavern as a hideout, and it earned the nickname Robbers Roost. Afterward, many curious travelers came from faraway to peer into its depths and wonder what villainous deeds those outlaws had accomplished.

The hotel and garden in early years.

Sometime after the Civil War, a 16-room summer resort stood at the top of Rock House near the present-day shelter house. It offered luxury accommodations, pretty gardens, and a view of the cave within a short walking distance. Then, people traveled once again to see the forest and rock formations far away from the towns and cities.

After many years, the hotel went out of business, the building fell into ruins, and nobody visited there anymore except to see the cave. It was around this time that the place where the old hotel had stood was rumored to be haunted. Passersby would see a ghostly woman walk from where the hotel's door used to be and make her way to the gardens, now overgrown with vines, brush, and briers. She lingered there for a short time, then faded away.

The shelter house where the hotel once stood.

Vinton County

The Curse of Enos Kay

Timmons Covered Bridge circa mid-1930s. Photo courtesy Nyla Timmons Holdren and the Vinton County Historical & Genealogical Society.

Many years ago, between Ray and Chillicothe and over the Middle Fork of Salt Creek, a covered bridge ran through the Timmons Property. A ghost resided there that would frighten young couples either passing through or stopping to steal a kiss within its dark corridor.

Timmons Covered Bridge at flood stage. Photo courtesy Nyla Timmons Holdren. More images of the bridge can be found in Images of America-Vinton County -Deanna L. Tribe with the Vinton County Historical Society.

One time, as a young woman and man were about halfway through the bridge in their covered buggy, the top came crashing down on them with a hard snap! Above, a man's hazy face appeared and drifted down toward them. The horse bolted, and the carriage tipped, dumping the couple in the dark while it disappeared down the dirt road. Many couples had to walk home in the darkness, and their trysts were spoiled by the ghost. After a while, courting couples avoided that bridge on the road altogether.

The ghost's existence has been explained like this— sometime in the early years of the bridge, a young man named Enos Kay committed suicide there. A handsome and popular boy, he had grown up in the fertile farmlands and towns near Hamden and Ray. He was only in his teens when he fell hard in love with a pretty local girl named Alvira. She loved him dearly too. He would scrimp and save over the next two years, preparing for their wedding. The sweethearts would often sneak away to be alone, meeting at the Timmons Covered Bridge away from prying eyes.

Timmons Covered Bridge. Photo courtesy Nyla Timmons Holdren who grew up near the bridge.

But just a week before the couple would wed, the preacher at a local church offered a picnic. All the young people in the community excitedly attended as it was the perfect place to meet new friends or find a sweetheart amongst the crowd. One of the young men present was a newcomer to the area, a Mister Brown who was quite handsome, strapping, and charming. He swept all the girls off their feet, including Alvira, as he shared a piece of apple pie with her. In just one warm afternoon, Enos was hardly a memory in the back of Alvira's mind. Two nights would pass. Alvira's new suitor shoved a ladder beneath her bedroom window, and the two eloped.

Over the following days, Alvira and Mister Brown's exciting and romantic flight was all the neighbors would talk about even when Enos Kay could hear. He was heartbroken and angry, and only a week would pass when Enos Kay threw a fist into the air and vowed: "I'll kill myself and haunt fool lovers 'til the judgment day!"

Enos hanged himself from the very bridge rafters where he had met with Alvira. Only two days after he made the oath and died, the ghostly appearances at the Timmons Covered Bridge began. They would still be going on there if the bridge was not destroyed many years ago as a newer state route was built nearby to handle the increasing traffic from Chillicothe to Athens. Only the creek and a few foundation stones remain on private property—and the ghost of Enos Kay along with the bridge is now gone. The road is defunct and now runs into private property. However, don't worry. You only have to drive a around the area for a ghostly treat. If you are looking for a scare, the legend advises that Enos Kay will find any lovers who park in remote areas nearby and haunt them!

Where the Timmons Covered Bridge once stood.

Hope Iron Furnace
Lake Hope State Park
OH-278
McArthur, Ohio 45651
39.331976, -82.340552

Night Watchman

In the mid-1800s, there was once a furnace that processed iron ore where Lake Hope State Park now stands. Hundreds of men worked there, timbering the hills for the wood burned to make charcoal to fuel the furnaces, working at the furnace, or hauling the ore.

Little remains but the ruins of the furnace chimney. It is enough, though, to harbor a ghost. Sometime during the years that the furnace made the iron, a night watchman overlooking the structure fell to his death into the fiery pit. Almost immediately after, when the bosses would have their meetings in one building on the property, there would be several loud bangs upon the door. When answered, nobody was there.

It was not easy keeping workers during the night watch, too, as a phantom lantern would follow the path of the dead man's last walk through the building and disappear as it came to the pit. Even now, vehicles driving the state route in front of the ruins of the furnace have seen a dim light hovering in mid-air where the building once stood around the chimney.

Above: The area in front of Hope Furnace where the general store was located and where the knocking was heard. And, of course, the furnace where a lantern is seen dancing—held by the ghostly hands of the worker who fell to a fiery death.

The Old Town of Hope
Lake Hope State Park

27331 OH-278,
McArthur, Ohio 45651
39.331370, -82.339951
Town was across from Hope Furnace.
Olds Hollow Trail goes through the town
and begins across the road
from the furnace, near the bridge
on OH-278.
Trailhead: 39.330912, -82.341087

The Burnt Cabin

The old town of Hope Furnace and Olds Hollow Trail.

Just after the end of the Civil War, two brothers working for the Hope Iron Furnace company as coalers lived in a small wooden shack across from the furnace. One night, the building burned to the ground, and the two died within. No one thought it could be foul play as both young men were well-liked.

It was mid-November and chilly. Most assumed one or the other had started a fire to warm the thin-walled building by pouring into a tin bucket filled with wood, some lantern oil made of camphene, a dangerous but cheap mixture of turpentine, alcohol, and camphor oil. And it exploded. Not long after, those passing the area of the burnt building heard angry shouting issuing from the charred remains, but after a thorough search of the site, the curious found no source for the commotion.

Five years would pass, and in Tennessee, police arrested a man named John Slavens for killing his nephew. He was tried and found guilty. As authorities were preparing to take him to prison, his wife confessed that she knew of two others the man had murdered. It was two young brothers who worked at a furnace in Ohio. Her husband had robbed them of their pay, murdered them, then burned their cabin to the ground to hide his crimes. It was the two young men who lived at Hope Furnace. Upon hearing of the double murder, vigilantes broke down the prison doors and dragged Slavens to a tree. They tied a noose around his neck and hanged him.

Many years have passed, and nothing remains of the little burnt cabin in the woods but a few old foundation stones piled along with others. The charred remnants of its walls have long decayed, a pine forest with a blanket of needles lays atop, and anybody who knew the men have been dead and buried for a long time. Once in a while, hikers taking the Olds Hollow Trail above Sandy Run and across from the ruins of the furnace have heard strange shouts and moans among the pines. They nosy around, searching for clues of the unrest, but nothing is found.

The Old Buhrstone Quarries
Along OH-50
McArthur, Ohio 45651
(at Peacock Road)
and the backroads between—
39.256858, -82.498965
To about Stone Quarry Road
39.234789, -82.423563

Headless Peddler of Elk Fork

Downtown McArthur, built on the early buhrstone industry. In the center is one of the round millstones made from buhrstone.

In 1805, a miller named Musselman started a quarry after discovering buhrstone, a mix of flint, quartz, and limestone used to make millstones. It was on land between Chillicothe and Athens running beside Elk Fork, a tributary of Raccoon Creek. Right away, Musselman hired a man named Pierson, who later took over the business, built a cabin, and made the first permanent settlement.

A millstone quarry boomtown grew from the settlement consisting of about 50 families living and working in quarrying and making the millstones. The workers stripped the land, and the stone was extracted and pieced together to create a composite. The millstones became known as Raccoon Buhrs as the quarries were located near Raccoon Creek. Strange things began to happen in the settlement after a few years. Travelers taking the path that led from Chillicothe through what would later become McArthur and then to Athens started getting accosted by a ghost. Locals heard horrid screams sweeping up from a certain place just off the road that led into a valley. Rumors began that a headless man stumbled awkwardly in the area around the quarries.

Old roads around the quarries.

John Dillon was a shoemaker in the late 1800s in McArthur. One evening a neighbor knocked on his door and asked Dillon to repair the soles on some boots. It took some time as it was late at night and he had to work by candlelight. When he was finished, Dillon bid the other man goodnight, and the neighbor went along his way in the darkness.

It was not long after the neighbor departed when the shoemaker was awakened by a loud thud and then a frantic pounding on the door. Dillon pushed himself from the bed to find the neighbor standing there shaking. He had been running so excitedly to the house that he had tripped on the steps and fallen. He told Dillon that after he set out, a woman appeared before him that was forty feet tall. When he tried to fend her off with blows, his fists went right through her body. She refused to allow him to pass.

The ghostly tales could not be ignored. Even the skeptics who lived in the area knew what caused the haunting. A peddler often passed along that trail paralleling Elk Fork to visit the settlements on his route. Everyone knew him; he was quite a fetching sight to see as his face was framed in a "throat whisker," a heavy beard. He drove a new-fangled four-wheel buggy not seen before in the area filled with table cutlery, silver spoons, lace, and material for sewing, and special treats for children. The peddler was quick to win over the quarry workers and their families with his wit and charm. He made himself so welcome that the peddling man was able to stay beneath the townspeople's roofs for a few nights while he sold his wares across the settlement, up and down the rugged hills from farm to farm. Then, quite suddenly, he disappeared as if the world swallowed him up.

A hunter following a doe in a deep ravine along the Chillicothe-Athens path happed upon a clump of brush and made a ghastly discovery. On one high ridge of the quarry where timbermen had cut a great oak, an ax had been left behind by a workman when cutting down the tree, and he had not yet returned to retrieve it. The brush had been heavily trampled, and there were bloodstains on the ground as if there had been a great fight. On the log was left a piece of throat with hair matching the peddler's whiskers.

Robbers must have ambushed the peddler and cut off his head with the ax, an easier route as one local offered —"they were afeared to shoot on account of the rifle crack—they've brained him and to make sure of the job axed his head off." Later, they found the wheels of his buggy in the deep ravine.

Macedonia Church
McArthur, Ohio 45651

The Devil Went Down to Vinton County

The alter at Macedonia Church.

Macedonia Church.

The Devil went down to Vinton County. And he just might have been looking for a soul to steal. He did not get one. At least that is what was printed in The Hocking Sentinel, February 11, 1886 about the Macedonia Church Revival:

> *"During service at Macedonia church, in their recent revival, the devil appeared in person before the alter, and when spoke to would not answer or leave till prayer was offered. He was a giant in size and had hands with claws like an eagle, and head and horns like a Texas steer, and as black as coal." Hocking Sentinel., February 11, 1886. Local Items.*

Lake Rupert
Wellston Wildlife Area
Hamden, Ohio 45634
39.20530, -82.53670

Great Ball of Fire

Near the brushy shores of Lake Rupert just outside of Hamden, a man was buried, and passersby could hear his ghostly footsteps walking along an old bridge. If you followed at midnight, you would see a ball of fire above the grave.

Infirmary Road
66176-66634 Infirmary Road
McArthur, Ohio 45651
39.273162,-82.441921

Hair-raising Hitchhiker

This little section of Vinton County not far from Moonville Station probably does not look much different now than it did in the late 1800s. There were a couple of farms here along the road by the fence. Alonzo Eckleberry was heading out of Zaleski, and when he came right through this same stretch of road, he had a ghost jump on the back of his horse and hitch a ride to the top of the hill. I measured it out to see how far the poor guy rode, and it was about two minutes by car. I figured it was a lot quicker on horseback with a ghost on back!

The Old Ghost Towns Along the Rail Trail

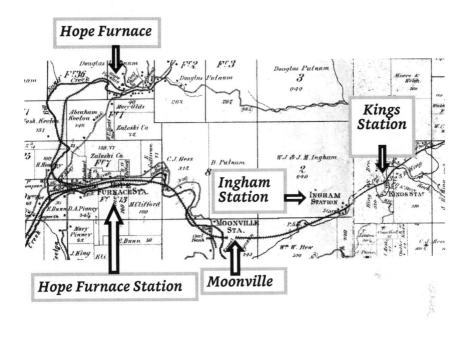

Hope Furnace

Hope Furnace Station

Moonville

Ingham Station

Kings Station

Moonville Tunnel
Hope-Moonville Road
New Marshfield, Ohio 45766
Tunnel: 39.307223, -82.322165
Trailhead Parking:
39.308039, -82.323823

Moonville Tunnel Ghosts—Lavender Lady

There was once a small coal mining community along the Marietta and Cincinnati Railroad called Moonville. Just a few homes were within the town proper; most of the workers lived in the surrounding villages and traveled by foot to work. In the mid-1800s, many logging, coal mining, and iron furnace operations had opened up in the region. When work was sparse in one area, the laborers commuted to other jobs nearby.

Right through the center of Moonville, there was a long trestle over a creek, and nearby, a tunnel dug through one particularly high hill to make a path for trains. Leading up to the tunnel on either side, there were continuing cuts in the hill, making long passageways of narrow, cliff-like walls. The trestle, tunnel, tracks, cuts, and trains became the perfect mix for many deaths in Moonville. Being tucked deep into the rugged and hilly forest, those living in the area used the more direct route along the railway to avoid climbing the hills to get to and from work or from one town to the next. Some were not quick enough to cross the trestle or pass through the tunnel and cuts when a train careened past. They met their deaths between wheel and track.

There was an old woman who lived in a little house not far from Moonville. One day, while she was walking the tracks, she was hit on the trestle and dragged clear to Moonville Tunnel before the train could come to a stop. After, her ghost would walk from the train trestle through the tunnel and disappear on the other side, but not without a warning she was coming.

In the 1800s, perfumes were not usually applied directly to the skin as they are today. Instead, women blotted rose, lemon, or lavender botanicals on kerchiefs or clothing, unless they were using the oils as a rubbing salve to remedy aches and pains. Some believe that lavender was the particular oil the old woman had used as a perfume or massaged on her aching elbows or knees that fateful day prior to taking her last journey. Because before her ghost would pass by, startled bystanders would catch the heavy scent of lavender wafting in the air, and some still do!

Moonville Tunnel
Hope-Moonville Road
New Marshfield, Ohio 45766
Tunnel: 39.307223, -82.322165
Trailhead Parking:
39.308039, -82.323823

Moonville Tunnel Ghosts—Engineer

Theodore Lawhead was an engineer for the Marietta and Cincinnati railroad company that ran through southeastern Ohio towns like Marietta, Chillicothe, Kings Station, Ingham Station, and Moonville. The route he took cut a path through Ohio's wildest terrains and had many tunnels and trestles. Both eastbound and westbound trains shared a single track with passing areas.

One November night in 1880, while Lawhead was heading through southern Ohio, the dispatch failed to notify the eastbound train of the westbound's route and time. The two collided near Moonville Tunnel, and Lawhead and his fireman died instantly. After the wreck, many of the trainmen feared going along that stretch of the railroad. They said they would see the flicker of lantern light when they came along a certain section of the tracks near the tunnel in Moonville. As they got closer, a robed figure would join the flicker of lantern light and step out toward the train before vanishing.

Moonville Tunnel
Hope-Moonville Road
New Marshfield, Ohio 45766
Tunnel: 39.307223, -82.322165
Trailhead Parking:
39.308039, -82.323823

Moonville Tunnel Ghosts—The Bully

David "Baldie" Keeton was a farmer who lived in the area of Hope Furnace Station and Moonville for a long, long time. He was 65-years-old in 1886 and still as big and stalwart as he had been as a young man. Everybody knew Baldie's temperamental nature. He was a bully who beat his wife and picked on anyone smaller than his size.

When he went to the local bar, he liked to pick out the littlest man in the room and give him a bear hug so hard that the other man could not breathe, and eventually, it would knock him out. Nobody wanted to be around Baldie, and certainly, nobody wanted to make him cross.

One evening, after returning from a court appearance in Zaleski, Baldie stopped off at the bar. He got drunk then got into a barroom brawl. He lost the fight, and the owner of the bar told him to leave town or else. He did leave, but Baldie did not make it far. When he did not return home, his wife assumed that he had gotten drunk and was sleeping it off with nearby family. When he did not contact anyone for a couple of days, she sent out a party to search for him. They found his mangled corpse on the tracks. Most everyone from Hope Furnace to Mineral believed he was dead long before the first, second, and third train hit him, and they were glad for it even if they did not say it aloud.

Mothers in the vicinity would warn their children not to go near the tracks and not stay out after dark. If they did, old Baldie Keeton might get them. It seems that his ghost was often seen hunched over and shuffling drunkenly along the railroad between Zaleski and Moonville Tunnel, grumbling to himself. He is also spotted above the tunnel, standing still and solitary and known to throw rocks and pebbles at those walking beneath.

**Bear Hollow near
Ingham Station**
New Marshfield, Ohio 45766
39.308678, -82.305132
Trailhead Parking:
39.308039, -82.323823
Trail may be impassable because you
must cross Raccoon Creek several times.

Moonville Tunnel Ghosts—
Still Looking for His Hand

What remains of the tracks.

The last time anybody saw middle-aged coalminer Allan Albaugh was Saturday, August 24th, 1907. He had been drinking when he hopped on a train at Zaleski with a jug of whiskey in his hand and heading for his home in Luhrig near Athens. For several days, nobody heard from him, so a search party was sent out to find him. Soon enough, they discovered his hand near Moonville Tunnel.

While walking the tracks at Bear Hollow near Ingham Station, Frank McWhorter smelled something dead and found the rest of Albaugh rotted and covered in maggots. Later, some who walked the railroad from Moonville to Ingham Station said they saw a one-handed man walking the tracks with eyes peeled to the ground. It was Albaugh's ghost searching for his hand.

Athens County

Kings Station
1157 King Hollow Trail
New Marshfield, Ohio 45766
Tunnel: 39.321380, -82.280123
Pull-off: 39.319824, -82.284548

Ghost Town Ghost

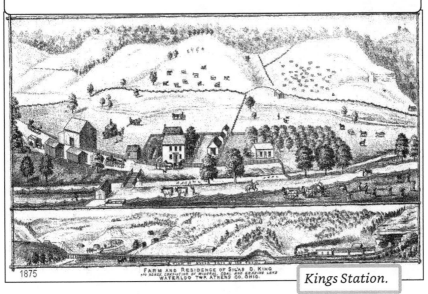

1875 · FARM AND RESIDENCE OF SILAS D. KING · WATERLOO TWP. ATHENS CO. OHIO.

Kings Station.

The Marietta and Cincinnati railroad was built in the 1850s and ran through larger southeastern Ohio towns like Athens, Marietta, and Chillicothe. Between, many then-isolated landowners gave the railway right of way through their property, knowing that a train passing through was a good investment. Not only did it connect them with other communities, but the property owners could also profit from resources their land could provide.

Towns like Mineral, Moonville, and Ingham Station cashed in on the railway this way, offering coal mined on their land. The King family also had land along the train route, and they were able to open profitable mines on their property. Soon a town was formed with a schoolhouse, general store, post office run by the King family, and housing for about 50 to 60 people.

Little remains today of Kings Station that you can view from the local rail trail.

Kings Station was not quite a bustling town by itself, but it became a part of a bigger picture. Because the train route cut straight through the hilly region much better than the old winding roads, many traveled by foot from one town to the next via the tracks. Kings Station was a central location connecting the larger cities of Zaleski and Mineral, so many passed by there, including walking within a tunnel that cut through a particularly large hill named Kings Tunnel.

Kings Station Tunnel.

This section, along with the tunnel, was home to a ghost. One night during a long week of rain and when the valleys had flooded, a young man set off on the tracks from Mineral toward Moonville to meet his father. Kings Station was between the two. About the time that he made it to Kings Station and its tunnel, he noticed an older girl in a white dress walking just ahead of him. The faster he walked, the faster she walked.

She kept pace for quite some time before suddenly, she disappeared. He knew at some point if he continued, he might have to pass her. Frightened, the young man ran without stopping until he made it to Moonville. The young man later identified the ghost as a girl with the last name of Hewitt who, just weeks after giving birth in June 1878, committed suicide by slitting her own throat with a razor to her windpipe. She had been married less than a year and lived a couple of miles from Mineral.

Athens Lunatic Asylum
*Now Lin Hall—Kennedy Art
Museum at Ohio University
100 Ridges Circle
Athens, Ohio 45701
39.320657, -82.109485*

My Ghost Story

The Ridges—Athens Asylum.

The old Athens Asylum is a familiar sight in the college town of Athens. Driving along the James A. Rhodes Appalachian Highway, it is easy to pick out the brick buildings just across the Hocking River and still standing on The Ridges, a wooded hillside just outside the town proper. It has been a solid fixture in the region for over 140 years— the building was a mental hospital from 1874 until 1993.

Now it is called Lin Hall and houses the Kennedy Art Museum for Ohio University. The building and grounds have been a great source for ghost stories over the years.

Building 26 was located on the hilltop. Touted by horror adventurers as the building for the criminally insane, it actually housed patients with Tuberculosis. It is gone. (39.323095, -82.113269)

Sometime long ago, I was driving my daughter and two of her friends home from a football game in town. At the time, you could visit the old asylum grounds after dark, and it was a rite of passage for high-schoolers to drive a certain brick drive leading uphill and passing an asylum cemetery before the road circled in front of old Building 26 that was touted to once house the criminally insane. There was but one way in and one way out. It was the practice to turn out the lights, making your way slowly around the circle before coming to a stop in front of the building.

One ghost story that stood out among others included the evil spirit of a criminal who would attack the vehicles. He would do all those horrifying things ghosts do to frightened teens in horror films. At the time, I believe, this ghost also sported a chainsaw. While he subdued those in the vehicle, the dead arose from the cemetery below to help.

They dragged those within the car into the forest beyond. Although we did not know it at the time, we would come face to face with this evil entity that very evening.

It was late at night and Halloween time, and I had just passed the main drive leading up to the asylum. A hushed conversation in the back seat of my car became quite heated. I peered into the rearview mirror as I had heard part of the discussion that went something like this— "So just ask her to drive up there. I won't let anything happen to us." The voice was deep, so I recognized it as the boyfriend of my daughter's friend—a high school football player who was still a bit haughty and high from a winning game that night. I looked into the rearview, saw all three faces looking up to me with cagey eyes. "You know I could hear the entire conversation; I'm two feet away in a closed compartment," I piped up. "But, sure, I will drive you up to the asylum." I did not mind. I thought that surely, it would be better an adult drove them up there than the three teens taking an unsupervised trip that might end like one of those horror movies. Since I missed the main entrance, I took a side drive.

As my car crept up the old path, the football player, who was sitting in the center of the backseat, threw a protective arm around my daughter and then one around her friend and grinned. I heard him cooing to them like he had a semi-automatic weapon tucked into his t-shirt to fight off whatever bad thing was ahead. I admit the drive was creepy. We rolled the windows down as we passed the main administrative building, then several living quarters. The air in the car grew oppressive as we bumped along the raggedy brick road past the old cemetery. It was silent, too silent. When we reached the peak of the hill, my daughter advised me to turn off the lights, cruise slowly along the road, and upon reaching a certain point to stop and turn off the car. I did and began to park when I saw something move.

"What is that—?" I started, interrupted by a loud grind of a chainsaw. In less time than it took for me to gasp a breath, the car was surrounded by an army of blood-dripping creatures running feverishly with a chainsaw-wielding, wild-eyed beast of a man at their heels.

A scream slipped up from the backseat of my car. I watched as the boy in the backseat, who had only moments earlier been a fearless seasoned warrior preparing for battle, peeled back his lips in a high-pitched cry and dove to the car floor. He abandoned the two girls desperately trying to roll up their windows and yelling for me to—"Drive!" I could not drive away as we were surrounded by figures everywhere.

What I did *not* know for probably the most horrifying four minutes of my life was that one of the fraternities had set up a haunted trail for different groups of students. I had taken a little-used backway on to the asylum grounds and we had happened upon it quite by accident on both sides. The fraternity thought I was the first car of their reserved groups to get there that night. They got a test drive and we got the scare of our lives. And I do believe that my daughter's friend stopped dating that boy the next day.

The building was eventually torn down. It does not stop the other buildings in the complex from being haunted. Those walking the grounds see faces peering out the old asylum windows like I did and caught on the photo above.

Old Athens Hospital Cemetery
Water Tower Drive
Athens, Ohio 45701
39.321825, -82.113795

Mysterious Circle of Stones

The circle of graves before they were moved.

The Athens Asylum has several cemeteries. The oldest is right on the asylum grounds, just a short jog up the hillside from the asylum's main building. Although caretakers carefully tend to the graves, many of the dead have little more than a basic white stone with a patient identification number engraved upon it.

People visiting the cemetery and hiking the trails around it hear groans, growls, and howls. Locals explain the sounds as this:

Once there was a section where the oldest graves made a wide circle. People whispered that witches made the ring, and for years, students from the college would come in the autumn to stare wide-eyed at the graves awaiting some horrifying event to play out, for witches to rise from the earth and dance about the stones. Later, believing that the headstones' placement was an early college hoax, well-meaning volunteers decided to end the shenanigans occurring around Halloween, dug up the tombstones, and placed them in a straight line.

Strange things began to happen after the volunteers moved the gravestones. They had overlooked that it was quite common to put graves in a circle around a monument and flagpole as a symbol of eternity and resurrection in early years. Those buried first received the honor of being at the most central part of the circle as legacies to the cemetery. After the headstones were relocated, those who were once beneath them were not happy with the intrusion of their eternal rest and the displacement of their marker. They haunt the old cemetery and those who visit.

Athens Lunatic Asylum
Now Lin Hall—Kennedy Art
Museum at Ohio University
100 Ridges Circle
Athens, Ohio 45701
39.320952, -82.109370

Strange Mark on a Floor—
What Margaret Left Behind

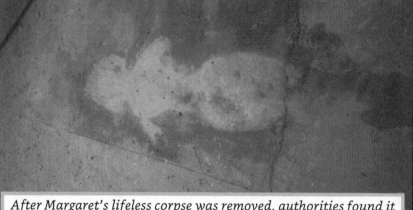

After Margaret's lifeless corpse was removed, authorities found it had left a nearly perfect impression of her body beneath. Image: Doug McCabe

The Athens Asylum has been known by many names. In later years, it was called the Athens State Hospital and Southeastern Ohio Mental Health Center. When it was known as Athens Mental Health and Mental Retardation Center in the mid-1970s, something peculiar occurred in one of the upper rooms that left traces of a patient on the building that still haunts it today.

One chilly day in January of 1979, a hospital maintenance worker, on a routine task, headed to an unused section of the facility, a vacant ward in the upstairs. When he opened the door to one room, a dreadful odor wafted out. Before him lay the decomposing corpse of a woman lying on the floor.

He quickly alerted her caretakers, who recognized the woman as 53-year-old Margaret Schilling. She was a resident of the hospital and a low-security patient who was allowed to wander about the extensive facility. The previous December, staff noticed her missing soon after curfew and performed routine searches. They assumed she had left the facility after being gone for several days. When found, the authorities established Margaret must have been exploring the ward, and she accidentally locked herself in the room. After caretakers removed Margaret's body, the breakdown of fat while her body decomposed left the perfect stain of her corpse on the concrete floor that remains today.

West State Street Cemetery
West State Street and
Cemetery Street
Athens, Ohio 45701
39.332356, -82.105851

The Horrid Tale of Charlie McGill

The grave of Charles McGill.

The epitaph states: *Charles McGill "Hanged in accordance with law" in Cleveland for the murder of his sweetheart. W. E. Peters.*

Mary Kelly was a seamstress and servant living in Columbus in the 1870s. She made ends meet as a prostitute.

While working, she met a man by the name of Charles McGill, who had come from a good Athens family, but his penchant for drinking and gambling left him ill-suited for keeping a regular job, and he worked off and on in the railyards.

McGill had a wife and children, but his estranged relationship with them mattered little to Mary. Nor, it seems, that he beat his sweetheart often when he drank. McGill was handsome and promised her a better life. But that life never seemed to come. McGill could never provide for her and later, after she had his child, could never provide for the child.

Several times, McGill asked Mary to leave her job after she moved to Cleveland. Mary knew she could not. She and her daughter would starve. On a Sunday night in 1877, McGill asked Mary to leave her line of work once more to live with him. She refused. He went out and procured a pistol and returned to the room at a brothel she shared with another woman. Then he shot her many times. When screams brought other matrons of the house to her door, Charles McGill was standing above the dead woman with a bored expression on his face. He lit a cigar and walked from the room.

Hanged. Cleveland, Feb. 13. — *Charles McGill was hanged in this city, to-day, for the murder of Mary Kelley, December 2, 1877. He awoke at six o'clock this morning, partook of a hearty breakfast, and during the forenoon took leave of his brothers, counsel, sheriff, spiritual adviser, and other friends. At 12 o'clock the signal, was given to bring the condemned to the scaffold. A cap was drawn over his head, the rope adjusted, and during a short prayer by Rev. Lathrop Cooley, Sheriff Wilcox sprung the drop, at precisely 12:04:30. After hanging thirteen minutes and half he was pronounced to be dead.* **Lawrence Republican Daily Journal - Feb 14, 1879,** —**Kansas**

West State Street Cemetery near the grave of Charles McGill.

Police apprehended the man quickly, and courts convicted him of the crime. The only words spoken by the condemned man on the scaffold were, "Don't make any mistake about that rope." And he hanged. In 1879, McGill was buried in a grave at West State Cemetery in Athens, an early burial ground for the city. A plain stone was placed above with the epitaph "Hanged in Accordance with Law in Cleveland For The Murder of His Sweetheart." Sometimes, people passing along the street would see a solitary and dark figure standing above the grave at night. When approached, it would disappear.

West State Street Cemetery
West State Street and
Cemetery Street
Athens, Ohio 45701
39.332218, -82.106115

Weeping Angel

About the time the first settlers came to Athens in the late 1700s, a cemetery was built on a hillside. Over the years, veterans from the Revolutionary War and Civil War would be buried here along with members of Congress, a baseball player, and even a notorious murderer. Some of the earliest headstones have crumbled away, surrendering to time and harsh weather. Nobody seems to know or care who was buried beneath them, except for one.

There is a statue of an angel at the entrance that watches over those whose markers are long gone. She is holding a book, and it is thought that she is writing the names of the unknown within the pages so that the living do not forget them. Those passing by have seen her weeping, moving, and even fluttering her wings. Orbs of light hover and dance around the angel, and some believe they work their way to each lost grave.

Tears fall down the cheeks of the Weeping Angel.

Simms Cemetery
Peach Ridge and Simms Roads
Athens, Ohio
Private

Specter of Simms Cemetery

Peach Ridge and Simms roads, where a hooded figure walks.

In the 1860s, John Simms was laid to rest in a family cemetery outside Athens proper. Old-timers say that he was the local hangman and over the years after his death, people began seeing a hooded figure hovering over his grave and walking along the roadway nearby. It was even rumored that the hanging tree he used was right at the cemetery.

Anthony Cabin
Hocking College
3301 Hocking Parkway
Nelsonville Ohio 45764
39.440046,-82.218075

The Watchers

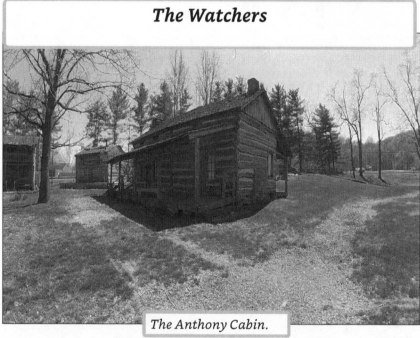

The Anthony Cabin.

There is a haunting in Nelsonville. It centers around an old cabin built by John and Martha Anthony over 190 years ago on land outside Union Furnace. It would still be quietly settled there along with its haunting if it were not for the Nutter Brothers strip mining on Loomis Road in the 1970s.

The company was going to demolish the building when they dynamited and bulldozed the property to get to the coal beneath. But the Anthony family, who had lived in the home for generations, donated the building to Hocking College in 1977 as part of a historical teaching complex.

The inside of the cabin.

The cabin is unique—a duplex found more commonly in close-knit Appalachian communities than anywhere else. It offered separate quarters for two generations of the family at the same time where the parents lived on one side and their grown child and family on the other. A total of four generations lived in the home since 1830. It is worth saving. There is a ghost. With all the mamas and daddies, kids, aunts, uncles, and grandparents living and loving and sometimes dying at the cabin, it was not at all surprising, even to the family, that somebody decided to stick around after they passed on.

It was not just the family who knew about the ghost. When dismantling the building, some employees of the strip mining company refused to help take down the home. They had seen the ghost on occasion rambling around outside the building—one even going as far to divulge that while he was patrolling the area around 2 a.m., he watched in astonishment as a tall, white ghost drifted from within the cabin and worked its way around the building. Another offered this up about the ghostly presence before the cabin's move to the campus: "I don't want to go up there and tear down that guy's home." But they did tear it down and put it back together at the college to save it.

It was not too long ago that folks would place an evergreen on the highest beam of a new wood home. It appeased the spirits that came with the trees, gave them a place to live, and made for less mischief for those residing there. During reconstruction of the Anthony Cabin on the lot at Hocking College, someone added an evergreen sprig.

It must have fallen off because the spirit shows up once in a while. Over the years at Hocking College, staff and visitors have watched as doors open and close on their own. Ghostly footsteps creep across the floor, and voices from the home's long past linger in the air. Sometimes, in the dark of night, a pale figure drifts from within the cabin and roams the grounds.

*Old Dew House to
Stuart's Opera*
*6 to 52 Public Square
Nelsonville, Ohio 45764
39.460148, -82.231858
To
39.460734, -82.231819*

Dead in His Tracks

Dew House Corner, Public Square
Nelsonville, Ohio

*The Dew House, right, and Stuart's Opera, far left in the early
1900s. Between, a place where a ghost has been seen.*

In the 1800s, the region around Nelsonville was a hub
for the coal mining industry due in part to the Columbus
and Hocking Valley Railroad rolling through the town and
making it a central point for transportation and shipping.

Like many small towns, it had businesses located around a public town square. Among them was the Dew House, an inn with a basement tavern, and Stuart's Opera House, home to entertainments such as vaudeville and minstrel shows. It was along the walkway in front of these two establishments, each on opposite corners of their block, that a murder-suicide played out in the spring of 1888.

Edward Davis was new to the Nelsonville Police Department. He had only served for 30 days as an assistant marshal. He was standing on the street corner by the Dew House around 10 o'clock in the evening when 20-year-old Samuel Dew approached him. Dew was a moody young man with an explosive temper only made worse by his heavy drinking. Recently, Marshal Davis had ticketed Dew for driving too fast. A day later and on this April night, Dew drew out a revolver, pointed it at Davis, and shot twice, killing him instantly, dead in his tracks. As he walked away, he said, "We'll have no trial." He got as far as Stuart's Opera House, put the gun to his head, pulled the trigger once again, and shot himself.

The area today.

Both men were well-known in the town, and the community talked about the murder and suicide for weeks. Eventually, time passed, the story grew stale, and most moved on to fresher news. There is one thing, however, that has not gone away. Bystanders hanging around the Nelsonville Public Square after dark have seen a young man dressed in vintage clothing strolling lazily along the sidewalk. He is alone and pauses at the corner of the old Dew House before he turns abruptly. Then he saunters toward Stuart's Opera and vanishes.

Luhrig Coal Company
Luhrig/Rhoric Road
Athens, Ohio 45701
39.336595, -82.179313

Screaming Hollow

Along Luhrig Road.

Luhrig was a coal-mining camp along the Baltimore and Ohio Railroad about five miles west of Athens. At one time, modest homes of the miners dotted the roadway. One night, a furnace exploded in one of these homes while a woman was filling it with coal. Her clothing caught fire, and she rushed from the front doors and out into the road, screaming for help.

Quickly she was consumed in flames and died. On certain nights, you can still hear her screams that follow a ball of orange flames darting down the street.

Mt Nebo Spirit Room
Sand Ridge and Mill Creek Road
Mount Nebo
Millfield, Ohio 45761
39.408410, -82.087197
On Private Property

Spirit Room

Mt Nebo. Early séances were held in a cabin along this hill.

In the mid-1800s, there was a cabin in a rural section of Athens County on a summit called Mt Nebo where spirits were contacted through séances held in a spirit room. The cabin was owned by a local farmer named Jonathon Koons.

After attending a séance himself, Jonathon found that he and two of his nine children, Abigail and Nahum, held a special gift—they were intermediates between the supernatural world and their own. They were able to communicate with the dead.

After several seances in the home, spirits instructed the family to build a special spirit room and add musical instruments the spirits would play during the séances. People came from around the world to see the Koons's séances, which was not an easy feat in the backwoods of Athens County, which required both a bumpy, backroad stagecoach ride and then a long foot trek to the cabin.

Visitors to the séances would attest that heavy instruments would fly across the room on their own, being in one section one moment and across the room another. Nahum would fall into a trancelike state and give information many thought too complicated for a boy of fifteen.

The Koons eventually left Ohio for Illinois, no longer providing séances. No one knows why they stopped late in the 1850s. Some say it was just too difficult to keep up their farming while others divulged Jonathon Koons's spirit guide no longer visited him, and he faded away in history.

Airplane Hollow
TWP Hwy 371 (Jacobs Road)
Nelsonville, Ohio 45764
39.527547,-82.247601

Ghost Plane

Mystery surrounds the military plane wreck in Airplane Hollow.

Sometime during the 1970s, the sound of a plane circling the town of Nelsonville broke through a violent storm. A couple and their three children living in a modest two-story home about 4 or 5 miles away heard it, as did the wife's grandfather sitting in a recliner in the living room.

One by one, all but the grandfather made their way into the kitchen to peer out the window above their sink and into the gloomy night. The engine's roar seemed to be far above their home before it faded away, then returned. Each time the sound disappeared, they waited for it to return, watching the lightning flash in the sky so perhaps it would shed some light on the mysterious plane. Suddenly, a muffled explosion shook the house, and the hills filled with light. Before they had finished stunned gasps, it was silent, barring the storm.

The mother and father rushed from the room, frantically grabbed jackets and truck keys, and made plans to get help. They had no phone, so they would have to drive down the rutted roads that were, most likely, flooded from the rains to get to the police station. Perhaps others had heard the plane crash, but maybe they did not. No sirens were ringing out. Before they could cross the living room, the grandfather, who was still sitting calmly in his chair, stopped them cold in their tracks.

"You don't need to go out there in that storm," he said, shaking his head. "It won't matter." His granddaughter was angered at his callousness and told him so.

"It won't matter?" she asked aghast. "But what if nobody else saw it and the people in that plane are still alive? How can you be so mean?"

"They aren't alive," he told her as he shook his head. "They've been dead over thirty years. That plane crashed sometime during the spring of 1941. Put a big rut in the hill when it hit it and took out a bunch of trees. I know. I've seen it. Everybody died inside. But the plane, it doesn't seem to know that. It just keeps coming back every time there's a really, really bad storm around here like it's looking for them or something. Like it's looking for those dead men—"

On May 17th of 1941, the strange sounds of a plane circling over and over outside Nelsonville overrode the roar of gusty winds during a full-blown storm. It was a desperate attempt of the pilot to find a place to force land in the gale winds. Not long after, there was an explosion as the twin-engine military plane slammed into a hillside outside town, ripping a swatch of trees, brush, and earth 300 feet. It was a military flight, and the pilot missed the field where he was trying to make the emergency landing. Five military men died in the wreck. Rescuers combed the hillside in the blackness of night with only the lightning, flashlights, and car lights to find them. It took several days to comb through the countryside as the wreckage was scattered all over the hollow and into neighboring hills.

However, the couple was not so satisfied with the story their grandfather had told them that night. The next day, they went to the area where they had heard the explosion and thoroughly searched the site. The only things they could find were the deep gouges in the hillside, now nearly overgrown, that the grandfather had talked about and trees still marred from the doomed flight so many years earlier—and a single, bent shadow near the roadway. They thought it was nothing more than a tree canopy casting an eerie shadow on the muddy road. When they walked toward it, the shadow disappeared.

They left quickly because the woman's grandfather had told them about that, too—"You stay away from that place," he said before they left that day. "Nothing good ever came out of that hollow. It calls things in and won't let them out. There's *things* up there you don't want to know about. Leave *it* be, whatever *it* is." They had not asked what those *things* were. To this day, they still do not know because the couple was too afraid to stick around the hollow to find out, and too scared to tell the grandfather they had gone to check it out!

Dawley-Downhour Cemetery
Jacobs Road
Wayne National Forest
Nelsonville, Ohio 45764
39.537182, -82.256467

The Place Where You Get the Heebie-Jeebies

In the past, the land that is now part of the ATV trails at Wayne National Forest near Athens and Nelsonville had little coal mining towns throughout the countryside. When the federal government bought up the land, those who lived in the communities moved elsewhere. Their homes, churches, and schools were demolished until little remained but crumbling foundation stones hidden in the weeds.

However, there was one thing that was left behind in each community—the old cemetery.

There is an ancient graveyard on a hill along Jacobs Road remaining. It is the Dawley-Downhour Cemetery and dates back to the mid-1800s. Although the cemetery is surrounded during the day with the growls of ATVs, the area is still controlled by those buried deep in the graves after dusk. People have heard the cries of a baby there at night. They complain of cold chills running along the napes of their necks, feeling as if they are being watched, and that heebie-jeebies sensation someone or *something* is getting ready to pounce unexpectedly.

Sand Ridge Road
Millfield, Ohio 45761
39.3943960, -82.1142460

Ghost of Sand Ridge Road

The place where Morris Claman met a ghost.

A ghost haunted Sand Ridge Road near the old county infirmary cemetery. On one occasion, Morris Claman, who collected and sold scrap metals in the Athens area in the 1890s, came upon the apparition. He was returning with a full wagonload of iron along Sand Ridge Road, and as he neared the cemetery, a ghostly white figure floated up beside his wagon. "I want to ride," it said.

Before Claman could deny him the ride, the being was standing above him and began to beat him mercilessly about the head. Claman rose and tried to fend off the blows, but his hands met with air. When Claman was finally able to draw his knife, slashing wildly but hitting nothing, the ghost disappeared.

Long Gone Hamilton Mill
Old Coal Hollow Road
Albany, Ohio 45170
39.199789, -82.117810
Private Property

The Premonition

Coal Hollow Road where a mill once stood.

In the summer of 1850, 17-year-old Thomas Bolin and 15-year-old Joseph Hudnall were camping out in a granary barn on the property of a local farmer named William Hamilton. Hamilton's teen sons, James and Wesley, were also camping with the boys. It was a common occurrence, these campouts with the four boys, and a way for them to have an adventure without being under their mothers' watchful eyes.

They stayed up late into the night, and then all four fell into a deep sleep. Sometime during the wee hours of the morning, Joseph Hudnall was awakened by the sound of woodchopping, and only moments later, a driver's voice calling out signals for his team of oxen joined it. Joseph, peering from his blanket, noticed the Hamilton boys were still fast asleep. However, Thomas was looking at him through his own blanket.

"Do you hear those sounds?" Joseph had whispered because he thought that surely, he was the only one noting them. Even now, he could hear the tap-tap-tap of someone hammering a nail to wood. Thomas nodded, admitting that it sounded like ghosts were talking outside. Joseph was somewhat relieved he was not alone hearing the strange sounds. More bangs and clatter ensued, and both boys set their eyes on the barn door.

In moments, a bright light appeared and basked a huge mysterious dog in its glow. Frightened but curious, the boys watched the ghostly dog. The noise got louder and louder as if the four boys were lying right in the center of a working mill—there was the noisy grind of stone to grain and steam popping and coal cars banging and getting unloaded. Voices wafted within, eerie and low, and then a low murmur not unlike churchgoers praying together hovered just outside the door. Right after, there was a thunderous blast, the creaking and shattering of timber, screams, and moans. The boys threw their arms over their heads to protect themselves, fearing the roof was falling. Suddenly, all was silent, barring the chirp of crickets and an occasional frog. The building was intact. Joseph was the braver of the two boys and tore from the building and out into the night searching for the ghostly, glowing dog. He found no sign of the beast.

Joseph and Thomas told their story to family and friends, who laughed off their strange experience as a tall-tale. No one had ever built a mill near the spot where they camped and probably never would. Mills, at the time, had to be along a rushing river to power the wheel to make the millstone turn. There were no creeks nearby. However, a few years later, the Hamilton brothers would build a mill in the granary barn's location. They could place one there now and far from a large stream because there was such a thing as steam mills run by coal that they could easily bring in by coal cars; flowing water was not needed to turn the wheel to grind the grain. They cut large timbers from their property, pulled them in by teams of oxen, and nailed the boards to make the walls.

Years would pass, and the boys grew older and had children of their own. Joseph and Thomas were the only ones who seemed to remember the strange happenings on that summer night so many years ago. On a cold January 13th in 1891, a now 46-year-old Joseph Hudnall felt a wariness settling on his mind when he awakened. As was typical, Joseph sent his boys to the mill, now run by the Bolins and called Hamilton Mill, to have their grain ground. But this particular time, he stopped his sons when he left and told them to get in and out as quickly as possible. The dream was lying heavily on his mind. "Do not stay in that grain mill. Get in and out as soon as it is ground," he told them. "That old mill is not safe."

It was a windy January day, and fifteen farmers were loafing about the old mill, chatting, and waiting for their grain to be ground. The boys did as their father bade them and got in and out quickly. Not fifteen minutes after they left, there was a great explosion. The men still inside were tossed outside. Edward Jacobs, who tended the fires that ran the machines, was completely caught off-guard. He died instantly in the explosion.

Joseph's sons hurried home and disclosed what happened at the mill. Their father only bobbed his head up and down because he had known all along that what he and Thomas had seen that night as teens was real.

HAMILTON MILL RUINS—The ruins of the Hamilton Mill, near Chase, can be seen in this old photo, the property of Mrs. Gene Stanley, Chase. Her father was one of the hundreds of spectators who hurried to the mill as it lay in shambles. What happened? Read the story for a bit of Athens County ghostly lore.

An aged image of the Hamilton Mill ruins after the explosion-1891. Image courtesy: Athens Sunday Messenger, November 10, 1963.

Millfield Coal Mine
Millfield-Jacksonville Road
(County Route 27)
Millfield, Ohio 45761
39.433264,-82.077608

Millfield Coal Mine Disaster of 1930

*Millfield Coal Mine #6. Courtesy
Little Cities of the Black Diamond*

There used to be a mine about a mile from Millfield run by the Sunday Creek Coal Company. It was called Mine No. 6, and many of the men who worked there came from Millfield and other nearby communities like Glouster and Sand Hill. The mine has been closed since 1945.

It seems like certain places can grab hold of great surges of energy that have passed through it, allowing them to relive an event time and again. This is what happened at Mine No. 6 and why people see and hear a haunting there. On a chilly November 5, 1930, temperatures had dipped to forty degrees with a mixture of snow and sleety rain. There were 182 men at the No. 6 mine site that day, along with five Sunday Creek Coal Company officials inspecting new safety equipment and four special visitors taking a tour. Like any normal day at the mine, the workers had gathered at the main shaft opening where two hoisting cages would take groups of ten and descend into the 189-foot pit below. The mine operated in double-shifts, and the men had just finished a 30-minute lunch break.

Suddenly, at 11:45 A.M., an explosion of methane gas and dust erupted at the back of the mine. It was caused by the accumulation of gas and the ignition of an electric arc caused by the fall of the roof carrying the trolley wire when it crashed into the rail.

Families waiting for news of miners. Courtesy Little Cities of the Black Diamond

Those near the front of the main shaft heard a slam, felt pressure like a descent deep into the water, and then heard whistling sounds. This group of seventy-nine miners were tossed about by a huge wind but were not injured. They escaped. Eighty-two men were not so lucky–73 employees, five officials, and four visitors were killed, mostly from carbon monoxide poisoning.

Remains of the Millfield Coal Mine buildings.

Some people have visited the location and say that they have felt the ground rumble beneath their feet. They have heard the frantic shouts of men and the pound of boots running. Nine hours after the blast, 19 miners were found alive three miles into the main shaft by rescuers. Although many believe the haunting is due to the tragic event of those who died, others believe it is caused by the elation and excitement of finding the men alive.

Pedigo Cemetery
Pedigo Ridge Road
New Marshfield, Ohio 45766
39.382813, -82.238062

Singing Children

Pedigo Cemetery sits on a little hill that was once the old Harrison Pedigo property. Its custodians have taken great care of the grounds; it is always well-tended. Someone told me that little children haunt the cemetery, so long ago, I went for a visit and walked the grounds. People often tell me of haunted places, but I do not always get a vibe from them. Here, I did. I quietly walked with a voice recorder like I used to do while my little boy, at the time, ran around in the grass.

I did not expect much. But when I got home and listened to the recorder, I got an earful. A young boy's voice sang quite clearly, "I am, I am, I am a lunatic." And I have no clue why a child would sing that—it almost sounded like an old children's rhyme.

My son, who was probably about two or three at the time, kept running up and down the steep, grassy hill. In his hand, he was holding a digital recorder because he insisted on helping me out while I took pictures. I told him repeatedly not to run down the steep hill because he was going to fall. Of course, being two or three-years-old, he giggled mischievously and did not listen. That evening I listened to the recorder and heard myself telling him, "You better not run down that hill." I could hear him huffing, puffing, and giggling as his chubby little legs ran toward the incline. Then a ghostly young boy's voice piped up in the same kind of warning tone of a big brother, "You better listen to your mommy."

On the day I went with my son to Pedigo Cemetery, he kept running up and down the hill. In his hand (as you can see now), he was holding a digital recorder. I told him over and over not to run down the steep hill. He was going to fall. When I listened to the recorder later, a child's voice could be heard saying: "You better listen to your mommy."

Concord Church Cemetery
12272 Concord Church Road
Glouster, Ohio 45732
39.450891,-82.050834

Rockin' Gramma

Concord Church Cemetery.

The Wolf family moved from Pennsylvania to Athens County in the late 1700s to farm the bottomlands of the Bryson Branch of Federal Creek, and they lived in the community for many generations. There is a small church with a cemetery that became the final resting place for their dead. Passersby have seen the spirit of an old lady sitting atop one gravestone. She is holding a restless baby and rocking it back and forth. A ghostly lone wolf also guards the cemetery, never crossing the boundary within.

Perry County

Old Rainer Road
Roseville, Ohio 43777
_39.801986, -82.128742_

Headless Horseman of Roseville

Old Rainer Road between the towns of Saltillo and Roseville is a lonely stretch of buckled byway. Since the early 1800s, travelers along this route have reported seeing a ghostly piebald horse with a white mane and tail. A headless man rode on its back. The horseman wore a buckskin hunting shirt and leggings and carried a rifle over his right shoulder.

A traveling salesman saw it. Of course, nobody believed him. Then, 87-year-old William Dunn, a minister, and 46-year-old John Tanner, a butcher, saw the apparition in June of 1888. The two neighbors were returning home in the dark sometime before midnight. The headless horseman ran between the men, spooking both their horses. Dunn and Tanner were stunned and related the story a few times to family before deciding it was in the best interest of their reputations to keep quiet about their bizarre adventure.

An old-timer recalled how the story originated. In the early 1800s, a wealthy traveler had stopped at a local cabin just off the same road Dunn and Tanner had ridden. Someone murdered him in his sleep and had cut his head from his body with a blunt ax. Not long after, travelers along the road began seeing a headless man mounted on a piebald horse cantering beside them. The murderer, who lived nearby, was driven insane by the ghost's nightly visits and drowned himself in a creek.

After an investigation, authorities found the traveler's money in the murderer's cabin. The people of the surrounding community buried the money in a secret place and vowed never to tell anyone where they hid it. For years, the headless horseman disappeared. Locals mostly forgot about the story. That was when Dunn and Tanner, and other travelers saw the headless horseman. Most believed that someone had discovered the murdered man's money after many years, and the traveler's ghost had come back to haunt the highway until it was returned.

Otterbein United Methodist Church Cemetery
County Road 62/ Otterbein Road NW
Rushville, Ohio 43150
39.771940, -82.363330

Bloody Horseshoe Grave

This cemetery holds a mysterious grave.

James Kennedy Henry was a farmer near Rushville. When he was 30-years-old in 1844, he decided it was time to settle down and find a wife. Two women caught his eye—Mary Angle and Rachael Hodge. Both were pretty and charming, and James was so smitten with both, he could not decide which one to marry.

One night while heading home from visiting his sweethearts, he fell to sleep on the saddle of his horse. When he awakened, the horse was standing outside the door of Mary Angle. James took it as a sign—fate had decided Mary would be his bride. The two were married on a chilly day in January 1844. It was a tradition for the parents of the bride and groom to give them a gift they could use in their new life as a couple. The newlyweds received one handsome workhorse from Mary's parents and one workhorse from James' parents, so the two had a team of horses to start a farm.

Mary and James were happy together for a little more than a year until Mary died while giving birth to a child. In February of 1845, James buried her in a corner plot at the local Otterbein Cemetery. Distraught, the widowed man would do everything he could to forget Mary—throwing himself into his farming trying desperately to rebuild his life. But there was one thing James did not do. He did not return the horse Mary's parents had given the couple on their wedding day.

Mary's grave.

James took nearly three years before he would begin courting his earlier sweetheart, Rachael Hodge. During this time, in the surrounding area, some whispered that James had broken tradition by not returning the horse to Mary's parents after she died. Mary's family was having a difficult time making ends meet and needed the horse for their farm. There were hard feelings between the families not spoken aloud.

Rachael was only 22-years-old when she took James' hand in marriage. All would seem perfect except for one small thing occurring when James visited his first wife's grave not long after taking his new bride. On the back of Mary's headstone, there was a bloody red shape of a horseshoe! It was an omen that would linger in the back of his mind for many years. James and Rachael had four daughters and were married for nearly eleven years. The couple was happy, but the dark cloud of the horseshoe grave followed James wherever he went.

Bloody Horseshoe Grave.

Then the inevitable happened. The curse would come full swing. While working in the barn one Friday evening, he was kicked in the head by a horse and instantly killed. It was the very horse James had not returned to Mary's parents that put him in the grave. To this day, the bloody horseshoe print is still marking the headstone. Visitors to the cemetery have seen lights and even heard the sound of horses roaming around the graves. Yet, no farm animals have been around.

Fairfield County

Sugar Grove
Old Logan Road SE
Sugar Grove, Ohio 43155
39.620510, -82.552969

Dead Peddler's Ghost

A peddler haunts the Old Logan Road in Sugar Grove between Lancaster and Logan. It was right around 1815 when the ghostly form began to appear, scaring away carriage riders and farmers traveling this main road. Back then, Sugar Grove was little more than a few cabins dotting the wooded hillsides and not the pretty village it is now.

Pierre Bordeau, of French descent, made himself comfortable in a shabby little place by the road. It was along the hillside not far from the location the Sharp family sells pumpkins in the cooler days of autumn and around Halloween these days.

It would be Pierre's shack that a peddler would stop and ask for a night's sleep along his route. But over the next few days, those who usually bought from the peddler noted he had not visited their homes. Many believed he had probably left Pierre's cabin during the night, so he did not have to pay for his lodging. There were no signs that would call up an alarm of any foul crime save a small pool of blood found by a spring near the road.

Years would pass, and whispers always kept travelers away from Pierre's cabin. Nobody wanted to stay there for rest. It seemed the water in the spring tasted bad, and you know, they didn't want to end up dead. And there was a certain rumor of a ghost haunting the road and hillside, popping out at carriage riders taking the Logan Road route, which was the only rugged path that once ran a straight drive from Lancaster to Logan. The ghost disappeared at the old spring.

Of course, no one suspected Pierre of murder. He was considered kind-hearted and had caused no one else any harm. But on his deathbed, he confessed to killing the peddler but refused to divulge the place where he had buried the poor man. Authorities searched the area for bones but found nothing save a decayed backpack with trinkets and the old peddler's clothing. There was no sign of him until nearly seventy years later when, in the 1870s, owners of the property dug a new well along the hillside. Upon excavation, workers discovered a rotted corpse beneath some fieldstones.

The family whose farm was on the land quickly gave the remains a proper burial, and the hopes were that the ghost would find peace. But many years later, farmers coming through the area after dark still took a two-mile detour of that lonely spot on the Logan Road to avoid the ghost of the peddler.

Fairfield County Infirmary
Clarence E. Miller Building
1587 Granville Pike
Lancaster, Ohio 43130
39.739089,-82.588996

The Old Infirmary

Early image of the infirmary, about 1909.

The old Fairfield County Infirmary and Poorhouse is haunted. Some have seen an old woman in 1800s clothing walking around the building. Then there are ghostly voices echoing through the halls. It has been around since the 1820s, and many of the needy, ill, and old have passed through its doors. Some were able to move on.

Others, however, appear to have decided to stay a bit longer. While you pass in your car, take a look at the windows and the front yard. You may see one of its boarders lingering there before they vanish from sight. Others have!

Still-House Hollow
Old Foglesong Road
(Now Stringtown Road)
Lancaster, Ohio 43130
39.765138,-82.596688
To
39.738016,-82.598523

The Half-Calf Shade of Still-House Hollow

Old Foglesong Road, now Stringtown Road.

In the early days, there was an old trail outside Lancaster that began above Coonpath Road and near a creek called Fetters Run. At first, the road was nothing more than a rock and dirt footpath from farm to farm and then to Lancaster. Then the root-ridden path expanded so a lone horse rider could easily travel its course, and later it was wide enough for a carriage.

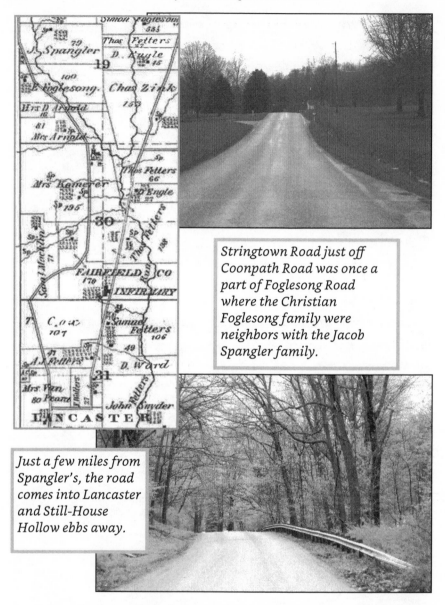

Stringtown Road just off
Coonpath Road was once a
part of Foglesong Road
where the Christian
Foglesong family were
neighbors with the Jacob
Spangler family.

Just a few miles from
Spangler's, the road
comes into Lancaster
and Still-House
Hollow ebbs away.

Back then, though, it ran a rugged route alongside
Fetters Run down through Christian Foglesong's property,
Jacob Spangler's house, and a few farms owned by the Fetter
family. It meandered past the rear of the Poor House Farm
and to the Van Pearce's who lived closer to Lancaster. It
came to an end where Rising Park is now.

Locals who traveled the route called it Foglesong Road for the family whose farm abutted a large portion of the road. They gave the small valley between the hills where it made its course a name too—Still-House Hollow for it was known to have whiskey still-houses hidden in the glens and ravines. Many strange sounds came from this hollow.

During these early days, there was a ghosting on Foglesong Road. Those taking the road began hearing wails and screams coming from Still-House Hollow. It was a place few would venture after dusk, especially in the cooler days of autumn. One late night, Jacob Spangler, who lived along Foglesong Road, was taking an anxious horse ride along the rutted road to summon a doctor for a sick family member. He realized too late that in his haste to seek the doctor, he had taken the shortcut route along the section of Foglesong Road that ran through the haunted valley. He halted his horse and shivered past his fears. He had no choice but to go on and so he did.

He had begun to descend the forested hill leading into the hollow when his horse made a frightened snort, fixed her front legs hard in the soil, and began to quiver violently. Spangler leaned forward and squinted into the darkness, making out a yearling steer in his path with strangely glowing eyes and long hair. He tried to urge his horse forward, but the usually fearless mare refused to budge. Spangler, deciding that perhaps the horse's judgement was better than his own at the moment, started to turn her around. But before the two could change direction, he felt something seize his leg. Upon looking down, he could see the steer was climbing up! Spangler was in such a shock, he could not move while the calf sat down behind him and placed his front hooves over his shoulders. There the two rode until the boundary of the hollow where the calf jumped off and disappeared into the woods.

Unnerved, Spangler continued to town and found a doctor to treat his family member. The two traveled the same route back to his farm. Partway, though, the same calf showed up on the side of the road in Still-House Hollow. It was the same place that a bloody trail had led years past.

A horse had come home without its rider, a man named Ornsdorff. Nothing was left but two empty saddlebags with blood and brains and hair stuck to it. A mob had followed the blood to the top of the hill and could see from the marks in the grass and soil where the man had fallen from his horse. They continued onward, following the path where it appeared the body was dragged from the road and into the hollow, continuing until they came to a house with a still nearby owned by an old man named Crowley. The doors were locked, but they broke through and resumed their pursuit of the bloody trail into a rear room. A foul odor of death and moldering sent some running out the door. When the rest threw open the door, before them lay a bloody corpse. But it was not a man, and instead, that of a dead yearling steer. The bodies of both the owner of the home and the dead rider of the horse were never found.

A Still-House Hollow ravine just off Foglesong Road about 2 1/2 miles from Spangler's home.

The Foglesongs and the Spanglers truly existed. There was at least one man named John Ornsdorf in Ohio, and one family was living in Licking County. Whether any fell to murdering hands, I could never prove. But the road was real (although it has changed its course and name a bit today), the creek is still there, and Still-House Hollow exists. The ghost, too, was seen by many. Someone told me that the Fairfield County Infirmary was nearly parallel to Spangler's route with the calf-like creature on his horse. Was there an inmate/patient at the infirmary who might have scared folks for years by jumping on the back of horses?

Still-House Hollow ravine.

You can still see Foglesong Road today, and it is only a short drive from Lancaster along Stringtown Road. You can take your car along the road that follows Fetters Run near Coonpath Road, drive the same trail Jacob Spangler took on his horse that fateful night he rode into the path of the calf-like man about the area of Keller-Kirn Park.

Maybe you will hear the screams and wails. You can imagine what it would be like to have the creature jump on the horse behind you and travel the rutted road until it ends about the time you get to Rising Park in town.

You can ramble along the old route, now made of asphalt and mostly pocked by modern homes and new county bridges. Nobody calls it Foglesong Road anymore. It went by Wagner Road for a while, then got sucked into Stringtown Road. It is not dirt or mottled with roots and rocks, and you cannot pause in your meanderings like old Jacob did because cars are rambling at less than idle speed on it now. But in some places, the land still harbors the ravines, thick woods, and dark spots in Still-House Hollow, like Keller-Kirn Park, where more than one horseback rider was terrified by the apparition of a half-calf shade and the dying screams of a murdered man.

Location of Old Mae Hummel Bridge
5210 Hansley Road SE
Sugar Grove, Ohio 43155
39.644941, -82.529426

Blue Flame Ghost

The Mae Hummel Bridge at its new location.

There is a small town between Lancaster and Logan called Sugar Grove with a stream that runs beside it, Rush Creek. This stream meanders into the countryside and, about a mile and a half away, runs beneath a concrete crossing where Hansley Road makes a sharp turn. At one time, the Mae Hummel Covered Bridge was located here. Sometime after it was built, the bridge and property around it had a ghost.

In the 1930s, a girl named Mary lived in the community around Sugar Grove. She was quite popular, always smiling, and known for her bubbly personality. Mary had a certain knack for making everyone around her feel good. She was surrounded by admiring young men, and many of them were quite wealthy. Mary had her pick of almost any man she took a liking to, but she chose a moody and loathsome creature known for flying off the handle in fits of anger. He was mean, rude, and a bully in all respects. Yet he was fair of face, and that is what attracted Mary to him.

The Mae Hummel Covered Bridge is no longer crossing Rush Creek on Hansley Road. However, the ghost haunting it remains.

It was not long before the couple began to argue quite regularly and all about the town. The young woman became moody and unfriendly. The smile always donning her lips was replaced by a sneer, and her effervescent personality changed to angry outbursts toward her friends and family so often, they hardly wanted her around. Still, everyone thought she would come to her senses and leave the unfriendly man.

But one rainy night in spring when the fog settled thick on Rush Creek, Mary left her house with a long knife tucked in her purse. The two set off toward the covered bridge over the stream that was secluded and far enough out of town that it was well-known as a lover's lane. But as they neared the bridge, the couple began quarreling even before he parked his car. In a moment of rage, Mary withdrew the knife from her purse and began to stab at the man sitting next to her. The two wrestled about the car, but not for long. Mary's sweetheart dropped dead in the seat. Crazed, Mary hacked off his head, pushed it out of the car, and it fell with a sickening thud just a few feet from the covered bridge floor.

She screamed as she watched it roll around and around, then as fear suddenly gripped her, Mary stumbled off into the darkness of the low-lying hillside ranting wildly to herself. Police found her the next day, sitting along the bank of Rush Creek, cradling her sweetheart's head and crooning softly to it.

Shortly after the murder, a young man took his girlfriend to the bridge. While they sat in the car, a fog began to settle on Rush Creek and then enveloped the road. As they watched it rise, a ghostly blue ball of light came rushing from the woods and stopped, hovering near the window like a face trying to peer within. The two fled but returned later with others. They waited in the car with bated breath, but nothing happened. Then one decided to step outside and call out for the girl who murdered her sweetheart. "Mary, Mary, Mary!" And with that, the blue ball came back! Still today, it is passed along that if you stand off the road where the bridge used to be and call out her name three times, a fog will rise to the road, and the blue flame ghost of Mary will sweep from the woods to confront you.

**Brown Bridge
over Rush Creek**
*Klump Road
Sugar Grove, Ohio 43155
39.637786,-82.472227*

Ghost on Rush Creek

The area where the Brown Bridge was located.

In the 1880s, there was a ghost on Brown Bridge over Rush Creek as written in the Hocking Sentinel June 17, 1886.

*A couple of our young ladies saw a ghost one night last week, near the Brown bridge over Rushcreek.—**Hocking Sentinel***

Shallenberger Nature Preserve And Beck's Knob Road
Lancaster, Ohio 43130
Shallenberger: 39.691446, -82.657781
Across Hunter's Run:
39.697388, -82.657265
And along Beck's Knob Road to:
39.701126, -82.657935

Old Hermit of Beck's Knob Road

Beck's Knob Road looking toward Allen Knob on left.

Outside of Lancaster, on terrain that was once miles of rolling farmland are a series of tree-covered knobs of Blackhand sandstone that mark the edge of the Appalachian plateau—Beck's Knob, Allen's Knob, Claypool Knob, and Ruble Knob.

According to legend, once an old hermit spent much of his days reading the bible and looking out over the farmland from atop the rocky hill of Allen's Knob. He lived somewhere below in the shadows between the two knobs of Beck's and Allen's. As the sun would set, he would make his way down the hill, whistling all the way, to the small hollow of woodland to sleep in a shack among the large rocks littering the forest floor. He bothered no one. And no one bothered him.

The walk home each night for the old hermit was here along Beck's Knob Road across the creek called Hunter's Run and trudging toward Beck's Knob.

For many years, the old hermit lived there. At some point, he became unhappy and decided to end his life. He began digging a grave at the top of Allen's Knob for himself. Sometime during the winter, he took up his flintlock rifle and killed himself, shooting a lead ball right through his heart. But before the hermit died, he left a note stating that he wished his remains buried in the spot he had dug atop the knob.

For years, passersby would often say they saw the ghost of the old hermit wandering down a trail from Allen's Knob and along Beck's Knob Road until it came to a bridge at Hunter's Run. An old Lancaster resident would tell the story of how he met the ghost one Sunday evening riding his horse on his way to visit his sweetheart. The young man came upon the hermit about halfway down the hill just above Hunter's Run and extended a hand, asking him if he wished to hop on the horse with him, and he could take him to his destination. As the hermit grabbed his hand, his fingers were ice cold. Too late, the young man realized the old hermit was long-dead. The two rode down the hill, the young man badly frightened and begging the ghost to dismount, but the hermit would not speak. Trying to dislodge the ghostly rider, he began to use his whip, but the leather strap went right through the hermit's body. It was not until they crossed Hunter's Run that the ghost vanished.

The Old Town of Clarksburg
Hamburg Road SW
Lancaster, Ohio 43130
39.685250, -82.618461

Clarksburg Ghost

There once was a town named Clarksburg two and a half miles from Lancaster along Old Hamburg Road. It had a schoolhouse haunted by a stagecoach driver who was murdered and buried near the building's side. Witnesses often heard the sound of a spirited stagecoach horse tromping its hooves and the tolls of a bell ringing. The murdered traveler was not the only ghost nearby. Along the roadway, a black dog the size of a steer waylaid carriages before it vanished from sight!

Delmont Road
Cincinnati-Zanesville Road SW
Lancaster, Ohio 43130
39.683857,-82.678989

Delmont Murder

The old haunted culvert on Delmont Road.

Fred Walker heard frantic screams one snowy January evening of 1897 near his farm outside Lancaster. He thought they came from the direction of the Hocking Township election house not far from what is now State Route 22 and Route 159, then Zanesville-Maysville Road.

Not long after, he thought he heard the sound of hooves passing along the roadway. Standing on his porch, Walker could not find the source of the commotion and assumed it was nothing more than some poor farmer herding in cattle or horses that strayed from his property. The screams were perhaps the cry of a spooked horse or the squeal of a pig complaining about the chilly winter night. A winter storm was upon the community, and it was too dangerous to venture far from home.

Days passed, more snow covered the ground, and the memory faded away. It was not until March and after a warm spring sun began to thaw the winter snowfalls that John Daugherty, foreman for the Cincinnati and Muskingum Valley Railroad, found a lifeless, decomposing corpse in the mucky culvert near the train tracks and roadway. No one recognized the stranger, but he was well-dressed and middle-aged. Someone had slashed his throat from ear to ear. Most assumed he was a salesman making his way from town to town along the busy highway. Thieves had brutally murdered the man in the height of the winter storm because they knew no one would be about on that cold night. Their tracks would never be revealed and cries for help were nearly lost in the blasts of icy wind. They stole his money, and left his body to be hidden by the oncoming snow.

Soon after the discovery of the body, a ghostly man with a huge gash on his neck began to appear. Carriage riders and even later, car drivers would see the mysterious man walking from Delmont Road to the culvert on State Route 159 before disappearing suddenly as a hazy mist into the ditch.

Johnston Covered Bridge
Clear Creek Road (County Hwy 69)
off McDonald Road SW
Lancaster, Ohio 43130
39.613445, -82.658803

Weeping Lady

The Johnston Covered Bridge was built over Clear Creek in 1887, and until the early 1990s, could still handle the heavy weight of cars. Those passing through have seen a weeping woman within the walls pacing back and forth along the bridge or peering out of one end as if she is waiting for someone to meet her.

While some believe she was a woman scorned by her husband and who hanged herself from the top bridge supports, others say that she jumped from her carriage during a terrible storm to calm the horses, only to fall into the swollen creek water below and drown.

This photo showing the ghostly lady in the background was taken at the bridge by Brian Smith. Tammy Smith and her son Jaron are in the foreground.

Shimp's Hill
OH-158
(Lancaster-Kirkersville Road NW)
Lancaster, Ohio 43130
39.762406, -82.617337

Headless Man of Shimp's Hill

Shimp's Hill.

In the early years of Fairfield County and about 1818, George Shimp settled on 88 acres of land in Greenfield Township, four miles from Lancaster. Along the northwest section of his property, travelers took a well-used road between Lancaster and outlying communities like Dumontsville and Baltimore.

It was here that the road made a large, c-shaped veer, for there was a steep hill with a difficult summit to pass. Some on foot or horseback, not wanting to go around this long cut, would go straight up one side of the hill, then down the other. Of course, this shortcut was off the more traveled section of road, covered with dense trees and a haven for thieves.

The hill would be dubbed "Shimp's Hill" for the owner of the land. In the 1860s, workers graded Shimp's Hill at its steepest section and cut through the earth for a more direct and safer route. Before workers completed the cut, a man taking the path over the hill and traveling near the summit was robbed and murdered. His head was cut clean from his body. It rolled down the embankment and into a dense clump of grass in the valley below. Old-timers still spoke in the early 1950s that travelers were frightened by the man's ghost staggering around the hill searching for his head.

The haunted Shimp's Hill today.

Leaning Rock
Clear Creek Metro Park
185 Clear Creek Road
Rockbridge, Ohio 43149
39.591450, -82.585024

Witch Rock

Just beneath a huge rock formation along the drive to Clear Creek Metro Park, you may see a row of sticks. It is passed down that sticks are placed there by area witches. If they are lying straight up against the rock, it is safe to pass along the roadway. If the pattern varies, or the sticks are slightly turned to the left or right, you may want to rethink the route you are taking. It is not safe to go any further. And certainly, do not move them. If you do that, bad luck will soon follow!

Baldwin's Inn and Run
1025-1041 Marietta Road
Lancaster, Ohio 43130
39.722016, -82.567385
(Private)

Ghosts of Baldwin's Run

The Baldwin Inn. It was torn down in the 1950s, but the legends of its haunting still linger in Lancaster.

Lancaster was once a central, prosperous agricultural region. Large swine, dairy, and beef farms were found throughout the area. These farmers close to Lancaster and even beyond were also fortunate enough to be near a section of one of the most major roads in Ohio during the late 1700s—Zane's Trace.

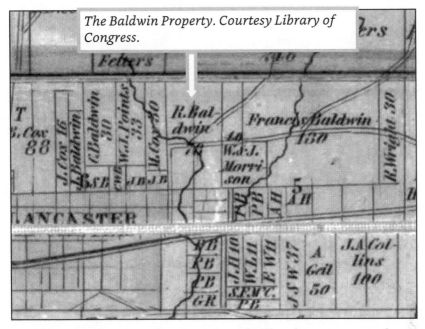

The Baldwin Property. Courtesy Library of Congress.

This major roadway was built large enough to accommodate wagons and farm animals to increase trade and settlement in the Northwest Territory. During the 1840s, a man named John Baldwin moved to the area and built an inn along the section of Zane's Trace in Lancaster, where it met with Marietta Pike to provide public boarding for those coming and going along the trail. The location was ideal, and word spread about the accommodation. The business thrived, and many came to know the inn as a place to stop after selling their goods and heading home.

But the inn's reputation as one of the best destinations also fell on the ears of a mysterious group of thieves. Those returning home with pockets full of livestock sale money or traveling with all their belongings to a new home became easy prey for a gang of local roadside bandits. It was not long before travelers visiting the inn became targets for the outlaws along the dark roadway.

Yet, the poor souls did not just get robbed; word would have gotten around too quickly where the thievery was occurring. Instead, the mysterious group of outlaws murdered their victims so no one would know the location that they had disappeared. The thieves buried the bodies around the acres of Baldwin's Inn and vanished into the night.

One night, someone murdered a farmer staying in the inn inside his room in the home's northwest corner. After, travelers staying at the Baldwin's related hearing bumps and bangs of the dead man moving around. Owners could never scrub away the bloody stain of the farmer's body on the floor. The inn was completely demolished in the mid-1900s to make way for new homes. Now only huge pine trees, tangled growth of underbrush, and power lines cover the low-dipping hillside near a newer home.

Of course, beneath the earth, there still lay the bones of those murdered along the roads around old Baldwin's Run. The ghosts of the murdered travelers still pop up once in a while and are caught in the headlights of cars passing by.

The area where the old inn stood as it appears today— between Marietta Road and Pleasantville Road.

Jackson County

Berlin Crossroads
OH-327
Wellston, Ohio 45692
Town: 39.084688, -82.537804

Old Warwick

Into the late 1800s, there was an old mansion known to be quite haunted in Berlin Crossroads. In 1894, a terrible storm swept through Ohio, and in its wake, lightning caught it afire and destroyed the ancient home. Originally built by Robert Warwick, the son of an English Lord, he ran out of funds to pay his workmen just as the structure was almost finished and declared he would finish it himself.

But only days into construction, he grew sick, and for months, he lay in bed until creditors took back the home. Warwick never recovered. But in his last dying breaths, he rose from his bed and paced the room madly, wailing and screaming curses on the building and anyone who would later live in it. Afterward, no one would buy it fearing the curse. Neighbors walked far around it in passing, declaring the dead man in the pallor of death peered out the windows at them.

Years passed, and then came the storm and the terrible fire. But when the mansion went ablaze, those who watched the fire dance along the walls heard the voice of Robert Warwick, watched him standing in flames shaking his fist toward the sky. He was wailing and screaming curses into the air until his apparition vanished into the fire.

Fairmount Cemetery
Fairmount Street
Jackson, Ohio 45640
39.057817, -82.623438

Jimtown Ghost

The citizens of Jamestown are seeing a ghost. Not any of your airy nothings, but a regular out-and-out spook—one of the kind that it makes little boy's hair stand erect to tell about. This ghost dresses in white, and stalks about scaring people almost into spasms. It is said to be the spook of a well known citizen, now dead, and to come nightly from the new cemetery. We would mildly suggest to our Jimtown friends that no well regulated ghost can stand a load of bird shot without materializing on the spot. One load fired into the ghost will spoil that ghost story. The Jackson standard., (Jackson, Ohio) Oct 06, 1881. A Spook!

The Harvey Wells House
407 East A Street
Wellston, Ohio 45692
39.124309, -82.530183

The Old Haunted House

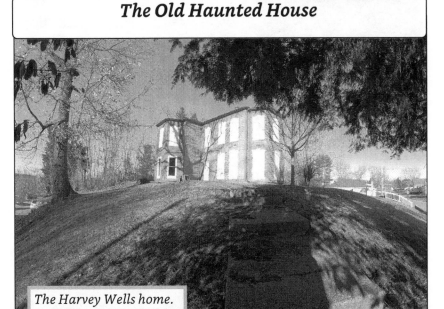

The Harvey Wells home.

There is a haunted house sitting atop a hill in Wellston. It is old and has changed hands over the years, but the two-story once belonged to the town founder Harvey Wells who brought the coal mining and furnace industry to the community. He had the forethought of having them operate independently of the city, such if they failed, the town could still endure. And it does still survive today.

In the autumn of 1896, Wells fell ill. In October of that year and delirious, he jumped 18 feet from an upper window and broke both his legs and an arm. Three days later, he was dead. Not many years passed before people taking the sidewalk in front of the home began noting a shadow at the upper floor window.

During an investigation, digital recordings exposed footsteps and a moan. There was also a clear voice of someone calling "James" —

It would become a nursing home for a period, and staff and workers could hear ghostly footsteps upstairs in the dead of night walking back and forth. Most believed it to be Harvey Wells striding across the floor before he took his life. However, there was also another death in the home in 1936. A man named James lived in the house, and before he died, he suffered agonizing stomach aches. Family members recalled him constantly pacing the floor to relieve the pain.

Lake Alma State Park
422 Lake Alma Road
Wellston, Ohio 45634
39.145796, -82.516293

Amusement Park Ghosts

Lake Alma back then.

Coal mining operator C.K. Davis built a lake resort park in Wellston in 1903 and named the park after his wife, Alma. There was an island called Davis Island in the middle of the lake and it was connected to the main roadway by a bridge. The island had a carousel, a two-story building with a casino/dance pavilion on the upper floor and food sales on the bottom, and an outdoor theater seating 1800.

The resort also offered a bowling alley, log slide, beach, a boathouse with sailboats and rowboats and a pleasant stone trail circling the island called a Lady's Walk. The Hocking Valley Railroad brought visitors to the park from Columbus, Jackson, Wellston, and outlying areas. It offered a one-dollar round-trip fare from Columbus. Huge numbers flocked to the park from 1903 through 1910 before the park closed its doors. Now the island is empty of rides and buildings and is part of a state park. Remnants of its past in foundation stones can still be found along with a few ghosts of amusement park visitors long-dead who haunt the island.

Lake Alma today.

To the left, you can see a boat filled with at least a couple of passengers who appear to be docking. There was no one there when I took the shots. Where the ghost boat appeared would be where the Lake Alma boat docks were located.

I was taking random shots for the book and got this image of a ghostly lady at the location where the large building once stood.

Salem Church Cemetery
OH-124 and Salem Road
Wellston, Ohio 45692
39.078658, -82.501895

Knock-Knock Ghost

My daughter and I both tried knock-knocking. She got a knock-knock back!

The monument honoring the unknown Confederates killed during a Civil War battle nearby when General John Morgan made his infamous raid through Ohio in July of 1863 is located at Salem Cemetery. Several of Morgan's men were killed when they crossed paths with Ohio militia on the hillsides of nearby Berlin Crossroads. Between 4 and 12 were killed, have been buried near, and haunt the cemetery. The church is home to the Knock-Knock Ghost. If you knock-knock gently on the door, you may hear someone—or something knock-knock back.

Pickaway County

Stages Pond State
Nature Preserve
4890 Hagerty Road
Ashville, Ohio 43103
39.671537,-82.936705

Down Under

Stage's Pond and the location of the ghostly horse team.

Sometimes when a storm rolls over Stages Pond State Nature Preserve, you can hear the deep thud of hooves bolting across muddy roads and then, the splash of swampy water as if something huge is bursting headlong into the boggy marsh there and being sucked down under. Afterward, terrified horses' screams echo in the air before they vanish as if swallowed up.

More than one visitor to the preserve has been startled by this commotion. When they ask locals, they don't always believe the truth told—that on a muggy August day in the 1800s, a farmer who lived across Ward Road was taking in the hay. A storm blew across the fields, and he ran to get out of the rain. Lightning bolted across the sky along with an explosion of thunder right after. The wagon team he was using to take in the hay bolted down over the road and across the muddy land around Stage's Pond. Straight into the marshy, quick-sand-like muck they went, mired and fighting until they sank so deeply down under they could not be retrieved. And now, only their ghostly echoes fill the thick air on hot summer nights, and right before a storm when lightning fills the sky and thunder rolls nearby.

Ross County

Mount Union-
Pleasant Valley Cemetery
Union Lane
Chillicothe, Ohio 45601
39.390504,-83.052692

Elizabeth's Grave

The cemetery with hanging tree to right.

There is a cemetery in a remote area and off a rutted, dirt road outside Chillicothe that is haunted. On foggy nights, a woman appears near a big, old tree at the rear of the old church graveyard. She walks along the perimeter and vanishes. Those who have witnessed the ghostly woman and taken the trek to the spot she disappears have discovered broken gravestones tossed carelessly in a messy pile.

The road to Elizabeth's Grave is remote and scary.

Among them is a grave with ELIZABETH etched into the stone. Some have thoughtfully tried to return it to its proper place within the threshold of the graveyard. However, by morning, the headstone mysteriously disappears and reappears in another place. The belief of some people is that a woman committed suicide by hanging herself on a tree in the rear of the cemetery. She was overcome by grief at the loss of her husband.

Note to the left of this image taken with an infrared camera—a zigzagging line goes from the front of the cemetery toward the tree. Was this where the headstone was dragged?

Meigs County

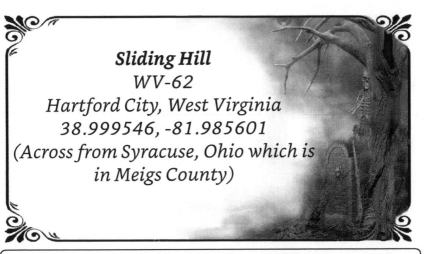

Sliding Hill
WV-62
Hartford City, West Virginia
38.999546, -81.985601
(Across from Syracuse, Ohio which is in Meigs County)

Ghosts of Sliding Hill

View from West Virginia side-just across the bridge. You can see the hill from the Ohio side, but there is a great scenic pull-off just across the bridge in West Virginia. Sliding Hill-left. Ohio River-right.

Just across the Ohio River from Syracuse, Ohio, there are two West Virginia towns. One is Hartford City, and the other is New Haven. Hartford City and New Haven are nearly back to back, about a mile and a half apart. You could probably stand between the two towns along West Virginia Route 62 that runs through both and yell loud enough for somebody to hear you across the river in Syracuse.

There between the two West Virginia towns is a place called Sliding Bend Hill or, for short, Sliding Hill—a sheer-edged hill that dips downward and causes the river to come together at nearly right angles. This awkward angle made it a dangerous bend for steamboat pilots as the water hits the rocks with such speed, it was difficult to navigate.

This dark recess had a ghost. Boatmen on the river and people traveling the roadways beside the river in Ohio and West Virginia reported seeing little lights dancing, ghosts, and even skeletons along Sliding Hill as far back as the late 1700s. In 1910, a family traveling south along the river in their houseboat anchored opposite Sliding Hill, unknowing of the mysterious lights. As dusk settled in the skies, the father began to see a strange light bobbing up and down the hillside. He grew suspicious of the light, silently slipped a skiff into the water, and paddled across. When he reached a position in the shadows, his eyes fell on a horrifying sight. He saw a huge headless monster shoving its weight into several large stones on the hillside just a short distance away. He made a hasty return, and in the dark of night, the family fled downriver in their shantyboat.

Reverend George Cleaton Wilding was a Methodist circuit rider during the late 1800s and early 1900s who traveled the mountains of West Virginia preaching. When he was about ten-years-old around 1856, he lived in New Haven and worked as an errand boy for a store in Hartford. George often heard of the story of a haunting on Sliding Hill. But even at a tender age, he scoffed at the idea of ghosts. Back in those days, there was only a raggedy bridle path between New Haven and Hartford, and one day, still in the early hours of the morning, George was hurrying to work on this trail. Before him, he saw a colonial officer approaching him on horseback.

The boy stopped and stared, mesmerized, and admiring the mighty horse and the grand uniform the rider wore, complete with a shiny sword at his belt. As the rider neared to less than 25 steps between the two and by a small creek of water trickling across the path, young George looked down long enough to jump across as not to get his shoes wet. When he looked up again, the rider had mysteriously vanished. So struck by the strange occurrence, the boy followed the trail to Hartford and found no hoofprints or sign that the rider had even passed!

The ghosts that step forth from twilight to the still hours of the night are those bearing lanterns to search fruitlessly for a hidden treasure. As the story goes, early settlers traveling along the Ohio River camped below the hill for the night. Within their boat, they carried many gold coins to buy some land. Unknown to them, thieves aware of their cargo had followed them.

In the dark of night, while the party slept, the thieves came upon the boat and murdered the settlers. They stuffed the bodies within a ledge and hid the gold coins until they could return for them at a safer, later date when suspicious fingers would not point at them for the raiding. They let the boat float on down the river.

Unfortunately for the murdering lot, they were all killed within the next year. However, on one thief's deathbed, he admitted to the murder and hiding the treasure. Not long after, the mysterious lights would begin. Later, many would search for the coins, but nobody found them. One by one, those who sought out the treasure were struck dead by some foul means and were cursed to come back in a ghostly form to search out the gold for eternity.

Scioto County

Fourth Street
Portsmouth, Ohio 45662

Strange Happenings on Fourth Street

When Halley's Comet hovered over Portsmouth, so too did a strange apparition.

Halley's Comet passes by Earth about every 76 years. In 1910 while it hovered within sight, it was reported in some newspapers that Earth would be passing through its tail and, as it had poisonous gases, it could be the end of human-kind altogether. Many people shut themselves inside. Others, however, dared to take glimpses of the comet.

On a warm May evening, Mister and Missus Turvey of East Fourth Street in Portsmouth decided to look at the comet. The two set their sights on the sky just above the home of a local hatmaker, Gertrude Carter, where the comet could be seen. But instead of the comet, the couple gazed at a woman standing suspended in mid-air between the two chimneys of the home. For a long time, they stared transfixed at the mysterious apparition before it disappeared.

Long Gone Street Car Tracks
2299 Ohio River Scenic Byway
Portsmouth, Ohio 45662
38.738997, -82.971133

Ghastly Shrieking

Looking North on Chillicothe Street from corner of Second Street—Portsmouth, Ohio.

Old street cars once ran in Portsmouth.

From 1892 to 1938, Portsmouth had a streetcar system, with one, in particular, running along Gallia Street to New Boston. On certain nights, a ghost appeared along the tracks, followed by a ghastly shrieking. Families in the homes near this section were often awakened by startled passersby who saw the ghost.

One night, Henry Austin took a quiet ride in his buggy along the roadway there when his old mare came to a standstill and refused to cross the tracks. He turned to his wife, who was sitting next to him, and she was staring intently at something on the roadway. Henry followed her gaze, and he could make out a man sitting on one rail with his feet resting on the other rail. His hands were settled on his knees. The man appeared to be gazing hard at something approaching, but the two in the carriage saw nothing forthcoming. Strangely, though, the couple could see through the man to the grass rippling on the other side from the wind.

Suddenly, the roar of an oncoming streetcar broke through the silence. As it rounded the bend, Henry tried to call out a word of warning, but the man did not seem to hear him. As the streetcar came upon the ghostly figure, he appeared to brace himself and tucked his head to his knees. When the streetcar blasted through the man, a horrifying shriek followed.

Henry staggered from the buggy, and his wife screamed several times and fainted. The horse bolted, and it took neighbors in the houses nearby quite some time finding Henry and the wagon as his wife had fallen into such a deep faint, they thought she was dead and carried her to a house before she awakened!

It was believed by most that the ghost belonged to 54-year-old Ed O'Connel. On a hot July Saturday in 1895, around 8:00 in the evening, Ed was heading to the home he shared with his sister on Gay Street after work collecting the First Ward school census. After his shift, he had spent his last fifteen cents on a drink in New Boston, and then he made his way along the roadway toward home.

A few hours later, Motorman Hiram Copley of the streetcar Edna was rolling along on a return trip. He saw something bulky lying on the tracks. After a short summer rain, the tracks were wet and quite slick. Motorman Copley applied the brakes, but it was too late to stop before striking the object with a solid bump. When the streetcar finally came to a stop, the people inside were horrified to find it had hit Ed O'Connel. The wheels of the car had rolled over his head, mushing it completely.

The area Ed O'Connel haunted along the old streetcar route.

Slabtown
(Front and Mill Streets Area)
12 Waller Street
Portsmouth, Ohio 45662
38.729691, -82.990130

Slabtown Ghost

Slabtown.

In the early years of Portsmouth, there was a large sawmill, lumber yard, and furniture factory along the Ohio River, with much of its logs rafted and floated down the Ohio River. When workers prepared the log for lumber, they cut the rough, rounded outside to square it. This cut-off was called a slab, and loggers usually tossed these castoffs into the river. People living along the shorelines around Front and Mill Street in town were known to collect these waste pieces when they drifted past; such the area was given the nickname Slabtown.

In early May of 1899, Charles Kirkendall and John Minor were making their way through Slabtown. As they eased down Waller Street near the Ohio River wharf, a strange mist began to appear before them. Within moments, they could make out a hooded figure complete with face and eyes. As they moved closer for a better view, the mist gradually faded into the night air. After that night and as word spread, bystanders often saw the ghostly figure. It was followed by splashing, choking and gurgling, and sounds of a boat drawn to shore.

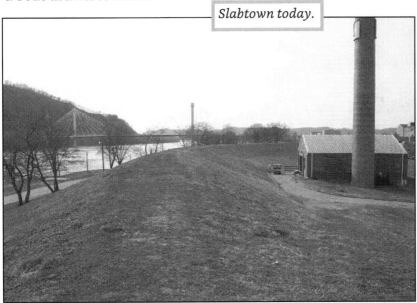
Slabtown today.

Some believed the ghost to be that of a little girl. One night, a woman with a child stayed the night at Weber's boarding house. In the morning, both left together to visit Goose Island. But they never returned.

2nd Street (Between Market and Jefferson)
Portsmouth, Ohio 45662
38.731666, -83.004245

Front Street to Scioto Street
Portsmouth, Ohio 45662
38.730860, -83.007292

Bridge over Scioto River
OH-104 N/OH-73
38.733110, -83.011746

A Phantom Story of the Scioto—
The Lady in Black

Old Scioto Bridge. Image: Portsmouth Public Library.

In July of 1888, in downtown Portsmouth, Nat Smith and Joe Henry saw a ghost. The two were heading back to their farms near Carey's Run about 3 miles west of downtown after making several purchases in the city. Their trek home would take them along the town's interior around Second Street, left on Jefferson Street until it met with Front Street, which runs parallel to the Ohio River.

Then, they would follow Front Street before taking a short jog north along Scioto Street, where the Scioto and Ohio rivers meet. There they would cross the Scioto River Bridge and work their way westward and home.

Front Street heading toward Scioto Street. The route that Nat Smith and Joe Henry took to follow the mysterious Lady in Black.

It was approximately 10 p.m. when the two farmers headed home. It was dark; even the moonshine was thwarted by the thick-leafed canopy of the trees lining the sidewalk. It was between Market and Jefferson Streets that Smith and Henry first felt a certain sensation of uneasiness. Neither were unreasonably superstitious, and they tried to shrug it off with nervous laughter. But just two weeks earlier and in the wee hours of the morning, a milkman crossing over the Scioto Bridge had happed upon the dead body of Portsmouth laborer Stephen Rayburn. The corpse was barely submerged in the waters of the river beneath the bridge. Although the coroner considered death to be suicide, marks on the man's skull appeared to have been made with a blow by a blunt object.

The crime, if it was, had not been solved. There was not a person alive that walked the bridge after that who did not take a wary peer over the shoulder where poor Rayburn had died and wonder if his killer was still lurking about waiting for the next victim. It was only a moment later when the ghost appeared. It was a woman, and she rushed past them in a swirl of icy wind that seemed to envelop the two. She wore dark mourning clothes—a black dress and thick veil covered her face. Oddly, as her feet padded down the walkway, the sounds of her footsteps were unheard.

The men watched in awed silence as she turned from Jefferson Street on to Front Street, nearly consumed in the shadows of the buildings. They hastened their steps, following the form that floated above the sidewalk. She turned then and swept up Scioto Street. She was hardly an arms-length away from Smith and Henry when she stepped onto the Scioto Bridge. There, she stopped where the middle span stood out from the water. She stared into the depths below, raised her arms, exposing a child within, and with a wild cry, tossed the babe over the bridge. She tore back the veil covering her face, and nothing but the sad, beautiful face of a woman stared back at them before she vanished.

The Scioto Bridge today.

Those who lived in the vicinity of the streets along the river or crossed the bridge reported seeing the same ghostly woman in black. Some speculated she might have something to do with the bridge collapse on May 21st, 1884. Missus Fulwelier was walking with her four children across the bridge when it fell, and three drowned. Others thought it might have to do with the murder of Stephen Rayburn. And yet, there was another conclusion. The previous winter, a mysterious woman had visited the Weber's Boarding House. She left most suddenly with her child and had never been heard from again.

Maults Brew Pub
Portsmouth Brewing Company
224 2nd Street
Portsmouth, Ohio 45662
38.731485, -83.008155

Spirits at a Brewery

Nathan Marshall, Brewmaster Assistant standing where a ghost was often seen.

In the late 19th century, a night watchman for the Portsmouth Brewery named John Keil was making his rounds through the building when a thin, pale ghost appeared before him, walked along the brick alleyway, and ~eared. It often showed up there between the brewery staurant, startling the unwary and still does once Sometimes another shadow accompanies it.

Dead Man Hollow
Grave Site
Forest Road 2
Nile Township, Ohio 45684
38.698616, -83.237139

The Mysterious Grave

The hollow and lone grave where a peddler was murdered—

A mysterious grave lies deep within a hollow about nineteen miles from Portsmouth. It is in an area of dense, dark woodland and in a secluded pocket of Shawnee State Forest, surrounded by a winding dirt and graveled roadway. The story of the grave goes like this—

In the 1930s, the Civilian Conservation Corps (CCC) was a federal program that offered jobs to young men to battle high unemployment during the Great Depression. The work was in parks and forestland and designed to open up these natural areas for public recreation. One of these sites where a CCC camp was set up was Shawnee State Forest. At the time, it was nearly inaccessible to the public, so among the jobs of the CCC were building bridges, trails, and roads.

One day, while the men were working on the forest roadway, they found a man's skeletal remains. Wedged within the crevice of a small rock overhang nearby were combs, implements, and tin plates—the type of things a peddler would sell. The bones were later moved and reburied adjacent to the little cleft in the rocks. A stone was set along the right fork of Twin Creek in the hollow to commemorate the peddler. It read: "H. T. Aug. 13, 1824. A. D. Dead M." Upon finding the bones, old folks began to recall talk of a peddler who, in the 1820s, routinely visited the rural towns nearby and who had oddly ceased calling on farms on his usual route.

Along the old road where the CCC men were working and found the bones. Center, is the grave.

They remembered hearing that a peddler had paused in the village of Buena Vista in Scioto County along the Ohio River. After selling his wares, he was directed along a 6-hour rugged footpath northeast to the settlement of Upper Turkey Creek, a community about three miles north of the town of Friendship. He never got to his destination. Most believed the peddler was ambushed and murdered, but no one knew the truth about how he died, or at least they would not tell. For many years, locals avoided the area of the hollow after dark reporting ghostly screams, whistling, and strange noises.

Dead Man Hollow got its name placed on the map after CCC began its project in 1933 making Shawnee accessible to the public building roads and the discovery of bones on the old Taylor property. Map circa 1949. From 1823-1824, there was a high mortality rate in Portsmouth from "ague" or malaria in Portsmouth.

Dead Man Hollow where the ghost of a peddler from the 1800s haunts the hollow and surrounding roads. When I went here, I found little pieces of plates and old buttons on the roadway. Were they trinkets from the dead tinker's pack? I will never know. However, I do know that on a special night program, several in my group heard terrifying screams that were not coyotes or bobcats!

Citations

Athens:
Philadelphia Inquirer 1889: Spooks and SpiritsAthens Sunday
Messenger November 10, 1963 newspaper The Athens Asylum
ballroom. Ohio University Archives, Mahn Center for Archives &
Special Collections, Ohio University Libraries.
Athens Sunday Messenger November 10, 1963 Believe in the
Supernatural?
Fairfield County:
-http://www.nitemarecafe.com/2013/09/the-clarksburg-
ghost.html
-Turner, Herbert M. . Fairfield County Remembered: The Early
Years. Ohio University Special Publications, 1999. The Lonely
Grave On Allen's Knob. The Clarksburg Ghost.
Shimp's Hill
-FAIRFIELD COUNTY CHAPTER of the OHIO GENEALOGICAL
SOCIETY. http://www.fairfieldgenealogy.org/research/resea.html
-1849 Plat Map—Fairfield County, Richland Township.
-Newark Advocate. Remember when-Shimp's Hill. Apr. 23, 2012.
http://www.newarkadvocate.com/article/BD/20120423/
NEWS01/204230307
-Shimp, Nicholas. http://www.genealogy.com/
-Eagle Gazette, Lancaster Ohio. 1950. The Legend Of Shimp's Hill
Hocking County:
Scotts Creek
-The Ohio Democrat., August 20, 1887. Deadly Gulf
-The Hocking sentinel., August 18, 1887, Image 3
-The Hocking sentinel., March 03, 1887
Old Man's Cave
-The Hocking Sentinel. June 22, 1905. The Wonderland of Hocking
Dead Man's Cave
-Logan Hocking Sentinel July 21, 1853
Queer Creek Ghosts
History of Hocking Valley, Ohio: Together with Sketches of Its
Cities, Villages and Townships, Educational, Religious, Civil,
Military, and Political History, Portraits of Prominent Persons and
Biographies of Representative Citizens. Page 1108. Inter-State
Publishing Company, 1883 - Hocking County (Ohio) - 1392 pages
Rush Creek
https://bridgehunter.com/oh/hocking/3732525/
What is it? A Question That is Puzzling Residents of Queer Creek.
Cincinnati Enquirer. December 10, 1887. pg 16.
Geology of the Hocking Hills State Park. Hansen, Michael C. 1975
Hocking County:
Old Man's Cave
-The Democrat-sentinel., August 12, 1909
-The Democrat-sentinel., August 15, 1907
-The Democrat-sentinel., February 25, 1909
-The Democrat-sentinel., March 28, 1907 Interesting Story of Old
Man's Cave
-The Hocking sentinel., June 22, 1905, Image 4 old man hid money
Simcoe
-https://www.nationalparkstraveler.org/2015/06/art-making-
charcoal-hopewell-furnace-national-historic-site26699

-The Ohio Democrat., November 29, 1900
Jackson County:
Berlin Crossroads
-Cincinnati Enquirer Author SPECIAL DISPATCH TO THE
ENQUIRER Sep 12, 1894 page 1
-Jackson County Engineers Office. Historical land owners Berlin
Crossroads.
Fairmount Cemetery
-The Jackson standard., October 06, 1881. A Spook
Ross County:
-Darby, Erasmus Foster. The Ghost of Enos Kay. Chillicothe, Ohio :
published privately by Dave Webb, 1953. Series: Ohio folklore
series, no. 8.
-Ross County Historical Society. McKell Library, Chillicothe, Ohio.
Scioto County:
-Harry Knighton, "Shawnee Forest," undated typescript, Digital
History Lab Collection, Clark Memorial Library, Shawnee State
University, Portsmouth, Ohio.
-SPECIAL DISPATCH TO THE ENQUIRER. Cincinnati Enquirer July
17, 1888. WOMAN AND CHILD.
-Andrew Lee Feight, Ph.D., "The Drummer's Ghost in Dead Man
Hollow ,"Scioto Historical, accessed July 1, 2015, http://
sciotohistorical.org/items/show/38.
-Portsmouth Times May 31, 1948 . Grave In the 'Wilds' Of Scioto
Co Holds Secret
Vinton:
-Athens Sunday Messenger March 11, 1923
-Republican Enquirer. (McArthur, Ohio) March 29, 1920. Vinton
County. 114 Years Ago in Vinton County History, By Our Route 2
Correspondent.

Made in the USA
Monee, IL
15 November 2023

46633535R00113